To Mo,
for more
than Morocco.

love Billy.

The Jules Verne Steam Balloon

nine stories by

Guy Davenport

North Point Press
San Francisco 1987

For my friend
HUMPHRY 1971–1986

Contents

Acknowledgments

"The Meadow" is reprinted through the kind permission of New Directions, which published it (under the title "Wild Clover") in *New Directions 50*. "Pyrrhon of Elis," "Bronze Leaves and Red," and "Les Exploits de Nat Pinkerton de Jour en Jour" were published together as *Trois Caprices*, in 1981, by the Pace Trust of Louisville, Kentucky. "Les Exploits de Nat Pinkerton de Jour en Jour" was originally published in the *Mississippi Review*. "We Often Think of Lenin at the Clothespin Factory" is reprinted, with permission, from *Conjunctions*. "The Bicycle Rider" was first published as a book by Red Ozier Press, in a different version. The allusions in this story to the Danish film *Du er ikke alene* are deliberate. "Jonah" was first published as a book by Nadja Press. "The Ringdove Sign" is reprinted from *Parnassus*.

The Jules Verne
Steam Balloon

The Meadow

• BLUE THISTLE

Here, said Gerrit, making an *iks* with the toe of his hiking boot where the meadow thinned out into the alluvial gravel of the shingle spit, *jo*? We'll be across the wind, with the *landtong* and inlet to see from the front of the tent, meadow and wood from the back. What quiet! was Petra's observation. She saw bee balm, and the grandmother of all thistles. Nello, easing his shoulders from under the straps of his tall pack, sighed, sagged, rolled his arms, and stomped.

• LA GARIBALDIENNE

Brainy steelrim specs, Garibaldi cap, Padvinster shirt with patches for wood-craft, swimming, hiking, botany, sewing, geography. Blue seven in a yellow oval on her shirt pocket. In boy's white short pants, big shoes and thick socks, Petra was straight up and down boy except for the flossy snick along the keel and the sliding look she gives you when she doesn't believe a word you're saying. Raised on Kropotkin and Montessori, she was great buddies with her folks, anarchists of some kidney. Quiet, said her brother Nello, hundreds of cubic meters of solid silence. Spiffing, our blue tent, nickelbright frame and yellow rigging. You can, Petra said, hear *mevrouw* and *mijnheer* Vole messing about, it's that quiet. Smell the meadow: clover, mint, grass, river.

• 3

Beyond the spinney there, back of the rocks, was where we camped, Gerrit pointed. Promised myself, I did, that if I came again I'd camp on this spit, with the meadow. Erasmus, said Petra, is nice but spooky. That jiggle in his turned-in eye, the flop of hair all over his forehead, shapely meat all over, but he's strange. Because, Nello asked, he lives with Strodekker, Nils, and Tobias? Of course not, Petra said, with one of her looks. I mean the way he talks bright and then runs out of something to say, fighting sleep. He blushes pretty. Nobody should be that good-looking. He's OK, Gerrit said, when you get to know him. Hans had told me that, and it's hard to fool Hans. It was his idea to winkle Erasmus loose from his tribe, his buddy Jan off to Italy, talk about a funny family. It was Rasmus's scheme that we not wash. Strodekker holds to a germfree nursery, peroxiding the depths of ears, crusading against dirt under fingernails and crud between toes. The whole house floats with shampoo bubbles and splashes with the gushing water of showers. Also, he'd had it with sex, said he was being kissed to death. Tell all, Petra said, but later. Rocks in a ring for the fire, the spit, pots and pans.

• 4

Everything's off somewhere else, Petra said, giving her hair a toss. We're here. The meadow's here, the river, the woods over there. Gerrit's wrinkling his nubble nose. Cornelius has the tent as shipshape and trim as a bandbox. Whistling *The Red Flag Shall Overcome*, she studied the page of the Boy Scout Manual that shows how to lay out a campfire. Dinky aluminum pots, she muttered, nests of cups. Water from the spring in the spinney. A sprig of clover in her teeth, eyes calmly honest, Petra edged her panties down. Pink butt, Cornelius said, soon to be tawny goldeny bronze. Gerrit, swallowing hard, politely stared. Prude, Petra said. Let's see what the river's like. And Gerrit in the fetching altogether. The river shines this time of afternoon.

• GOLDBUTTONS

Petra drawing plants in her sketchbook, saying the names of parts to herself, bract, umbel, petiole, said to Gerrit who came to watch, they're alive. They're out here on their own, as independent as Frisians. They were here before we were, I mean before people were, at all, them and the insects, so it's their world we're visiting, intruding on. Time is so grandly slow. No, said Gerrit, it's just that there's so much of it. What I like, Petra said, is a thing minding its own business, like this little goldbutton here. Greeny white roots, a hard stalk, its flowers eight to the line here at the bottom, five on the next level up, three, two, one. It's just tall enough to live in with the grass and still eat lots of light, and get enough water through its toes. Axial, but not strictly: you can't lay a ruler along any of its lines. The orangey yellow of the flower matches the dandelion green of its leaves: they go together.

• 6

Mitochondria, Petra said, cytoblasts. Everything may be a symbiosis of the two. Every once in a while, Cornelius said, my weewee goes weightless, floating. Because we're britchesless, I suppose. The earth, Petra said, was deep in bacteria once upon a time, making the oxygen for our atmosphere. Erasmus last summer, Gerrit said, called Hans an elemental sprite, or djinn, a hybrid of whacky Toby and serious Nils. The weeds out here, Petra said, are not weeds. This is their place, their meadow. Erasmus said his predicament was that his hormones turned on early, with the help of a camp counsellor, a buttermilk-fed weightlifter who believed in flying saucers and extrasensory perception, and told his charges that it was good for their souls to whack off until their brains were sodden. Showed them how, and lectured on the hygiene of it all. Some people, Cornelius said, have all the luck. Nello, Petra said, wants you to believe that we're afflicted with stuffy parents when we're not. Why then, Nello said, am I so shy? Look, Petra said, how plants make colonies, like islands, and don't mix in with each other.

• 7

Happy dimples and merry eyes, Nello said, is what Gerrit has all over his face, and Petra can't kiss for laughing. Don't niggle, Petra said, we're doing our best. Straight face, puckered lips. Close your eyes, Nello said. I'm pretty certain you're supposed to close your eyes. A squint will do, like that. Side by side, prone, Gerrit's feet riding up and down in a swinging kick, Petra's toes dug into clover, they kissed again, rocking their lips, Nello counting to sixty, one and abra, two cadabra. Nello hummed. Sixty abracadabra. A whole minute. Peppermint, Petra said, rolling onto her back and stretching. Gerrit walked his elbows closer, grazed Petra's lips with his, and mashed into another kiss. Both heels rose. He ventured a hand over a breast. Nello kicked into a headstand and watched upside down. If you like it, you like it. If you don't, what are you doing it for? Sixty and five, sixty and six. Two minutes and one, two minutes and two. Blood's rushing to my head and I'm going to croak in a fit. Three minutes. Gerrit lifted, but Petra pulled his head back, and kept her hand in his hair.

• LANDTONG

The feldspar and quartz pebbles derive from precambrian gneisses or granites and the small fragments of tourmaline and garnets from crystalline schists. The general inference, therefore, from the pebbles is that the beds in which they occur were uncomformably related to certain precambrian gneisses and certain slates, limestones, and quartzites of Cambrian or Lower Silurian age.

• SYCAMORE

The *Jules Verne* stood tethered in the spinney beyond the meadow, its yellow drag tied to a boulder, valves leaking steam. Its girdling panels of zodiac, polychrome asterisks, and Laplander embroidery were as benign an intrusion among the trees of the grove as a circus wagon on the street of a Baltic town, a flourish of band music into the domestic sounds of a village. Quark in a Danish student cap, American jeans, Lord Byron shirt with ample sleeves, was picking blueberries in a school of butterflies. Tumble and Buckeye had climbed into a sycamore, walking its limbs as easily as cats. Tumble sat, hooked his knees on a horizontal branch, and hung upside down. Well, he said, there's the begetted eightness of unique nuclearity. Sure, said Tumble, noneness or nineness, or there's no dance to the frequency of the wave. Quark, overhearing in the blueberries, shouted that numbers are numbers.

Zero one way, zero the other, scattering butterflies by drawing a goose egg in the air. The zero in ten is a nine pretending it's under one to be beside it and generate a progression of nine again. Tumble, parking his Norwegian forager's cap over a spray of sycamore leaves, said two four six, three six nine is what you get in a multiplication by threes along the one-to-niner line, but by four gives four eight three seven two six one five nine before you get to four again. He pried off his sneakers, tied the laces together, and hung them from a stout twig. Into each sneaker he stuffed a sock, white, striped blue and red at the top. By five, said Buckeye, gets you five one six two seven three eight four nine, which leaves a space between numbers for landing in when you leapfrog back from four to one. Quark, down among the blueberries, had sailed his cap to the boulder with nonchalant accuracy, and pulled off his shirt, which he made into a ball, tossing it over his head to land behind him in a patch of goldenrod and rabbit tobacco. By six, he shouted, six three nine, six three nine, over and over, out to infinity. Tumble upside down, squirmed out of his sweater, like a bat peeling itself, as Buckeye remarked, and let it drop far below. Bet you can't shuck your jeans, Quark dared him, while hanging upside down by your knees. Bet I can, said Tumble, watch. Unbuckling and zipping down, he sang, or zipping up, considering, I lift my left leg off the limb, so. And slide my left leg out, ha. And latch on again, squeezing good, with left knee while easing right leg out, and what was the bet, Quark old boy? He did it! Buckeye said. But your face is red as a tomato. Feel lightheaded, too, Tumble said, lifting his arms to the limb and scrambling onto it, astride. Woof! By seven, he said, seven five three one eight six four two nine. You lose two every step except from one to eight and two to nine, where you add seven. That's the best yet, Buckeye said, and with a bet won to boot. Think of something good and nasty. By eight, Quark said, eight seven six. Changing the subject! said Tumble. As for the bet, I was thinking. Eight seven six, Quark shouted him down, five four three. I was thinking that. Two! One! Nine! That, said Buckeye, has its tail in its mouth. The eight's on one end, the nine on the other, and the in-between's reversed. I was thinking, Tumble dogged on, that as long as my jeans are fifteen feet down, where, as soon as they're off, my underpants will follow, there, have followed, *whee!* right on top. By nine, Quark sang, nine nine nine nine nine nine nine nine nine.

• LEAVES

Wild tansy, Petra said, Roman wormwood. *Ambrosia Artemisiaefolia.* Not, I think, Theophrastos' *apsinthion*, which is *Artemisia*, genus and species swapping places as in a dance. This is a New World weed with pinnatifid leaves, very Greek, very acanthus. The flowers go on and on up the stem, shishkabob of yellow ruffles, tight little green balls when they begin. She leaned over the wild tansy, spraddle-legged, hands on knees, Gerrit's long-billed red cap on the back of her head. Carrotweed, said Gerrit, finding it in the book. Stammerwort tasselweed ragweed tall ambrosia. Ambrosia is what the Greek gods ate, and at our house it's orange slices bananas grapes pineapple and coconut wish I had some now. Nectar's what they drank and now bees drink it. I like being naked, I think. Artemisleaf, said Petra. Of course. Because it has a leaf like *Artemisia*, toothy lobes in a nineteenth-century neoclassical spray. You look good naked, long brown legs and big square toes. Botanists are nice people, gentle, with queer names. Sereno Watson. Blue-eyed grass, said Cornelius. Artemis was the Greek goddess of hunting and women and young animals. Women when they're young animals, said Petra.

• DOUBLE FLOWER OF BRISTOW, OR NONESUCH

This glorious flower being as rare as it is beautiful, is for roots being stringy, for leaves and stalks being hairy and high, and for the flowers growing in tufts, altogether like the single nonesuch: but that this bears a larger umbel of flowers at the stalk's top, every flower having three or four rows of petals, of a deeper orange, adding more grace, but blossoms without making seed, like other double flowers, but overcomes this defect by propagating from the root.

• SNUG

What I like, Petra said in the sleeping bag, is a dark sleety winter afternoon when I can go from school clothes to flannel pyjamas and wool dressing gown and get snug in the big chair with a blanket and something good to read, and can see outside. You've got so many worlds at once: memory both recent and far, the house with supper coming along and talk and Papa coming in, and your book. You know where you are. A cat's view of life, Cornelius said. Thanks, said Petra. Where we are here, Gerrit said, is the backside of nowhere, under all the stars, at the edge of a meadow, near a river, all three in two sleeping bags zipped into one, Petra in the middle. Straight down is New Zealand. Did you see the mouse on a stem of broomsedge, holding on with four fists? Petra did, but Nello missed him.

• A STRING OF SPANISH ONIONS

Candlelight in our tent, and every sound an event to itself, spoon's clink on a cup, and our voices. Hansje was happiest that we weren't going to wash, and kept saying we'd stink. Erasmus was cool about it. Take off socks, briefs, a shirt, he said, and into the laundry basket it goes. It's good to wear dust and mud, pollen and leaftrash. Hansje pointed out that we didn't know what dirty was. And, besides, naked and dirty was different from wearing dirty clothes. Places, Erasmus said. The meadow can't be dirty. I said that it could. Dump city trash on it, atomic waste, industrial crud. Understood, Erasmus said. But we, sweaty and dusty and with oniony armpits, are clean in the same way the meadow is clean. We're natural. What if we hadn't brought toilet paper? Well, Erasmus said, we have a river, and even dust. We could powder, like birds. Every culture has its own sense of clean and dirty. Every part of a city. Every family. But the day your socks are yours, comfortable and friendly, is the day parents snatch them away from you. Then Erasmus made a speech on dirt: which he said was anything out of place, like seasand in the carpet, dust on shelves, egg on a necktie. But it was Erasmus who rolled in dust when he was sweaty. Petra didn't need to say a word. Her eyes said it all.

• RISE AND SET, AUTUMNAL STARS

So, Petra said, Hiroshige. What's happening at a place. A tree, and it's there through the seasons. It has its life, from seedling to ax or lightning bolt. But it's there. And then, all of a minute, when Hiroshige chooses to have us look, a peasant carrying two bundles of firewood on a yoke across his shoulders passes the tree. At the same moment, a monk, a lady on a horse, they are also passing. Our meadow here was under snow last winter, and hares made tracks across it, and the mice burrowed deeper and all the grass and flowers were dead. And now we're here with our blue tent and each other. And last summer, Gerrit said, Erasmus doing a hundred push-ups at a time, counting in Latin, betting Hansje he couldn't do a hundred and five. And unmentionable things, Petra said. No, said Gerrit, that was part of the game. Pure thoughts all the way, like us.

• 1 5

The sleeping bags zipped together, as with Hans, Erasmus, and Gerrit before, Gerrit's plan, one less sleeping bag to tote, and, as Petra explained to her folks back in Amsterdam, proof of their freedom. Me in the middle, Petra said. Liberal parents are the stuffiest. If ours were a Calvinist enclave where sex is never mentioned except to deny its existence, not an eyebrow would raise at three innocent teenagers camping in a meadow, two of them brother and sister, the other a friend from the playpen forward. Liberals are the new Calvinists. Those Danes, Nello said, in Jugoslavia. I'm still trying to figure out what they were doing. Four girls and one boy in the tent back of the textileless beach. Squealed all night, that lot.

• PARNASSIA PALUSTRIS LINNAEUS

Flowers, fragrant as honey, are interesting in that five of the original stamens transform into staminodes split into narrow gland-tipped segments, which attract insects. The five fertile stamens alternate with the petals and mature before the stigmas, but in a remarkable way. The anthers face outwards and ripen in succession, each in turn lying on top of the ovary with the pollen side facing upwards. After several days, when the anthers are all empty of pollen, the apical stigmas become receptive and occupy the former position of the anthers. Knuth's *Handbook of Flower Pollination* says that the stalked glands of the staminodes attract insects by their glistening color, as if they had abundant nectar. Intelligent insects are not deceived, but flies and beetles are, and effect cross-pollination. Many smaller flies are also attracted. They lick the nectar but are ineffective in transferring pollen.

• CAMPFIRE

Minimal possessions, Gerrit said, maximum order. Last summer, Petra said, we had maximum possessions at camp, carloads of stuff, and most likely minimal order, no matter how loud the games mistresses shouted at us, as muddled as we were. One reason, among others, when Gerrit went off here with Hansje Keirinckx and Erasmus Strodekker, I saw that camping could be something quite different from a giggle of girls talking boys, television, clothes, and homework. So here we are. Nello will live down going camping with his sister. Never, said Cornelius. A knowing smile will serve, Petra said, if not an invitation to mind one's business. Well, Gerrit said, we're different. We have hygiene, sort of. It was Hansje's bright idea that we go native and swear off soap and water, as a corollary to Erasmus's giving up sex. He said one morning that waking up out here's fun because the mind's an idiot and thinks it's where it usually is when you wake, when it, by happy surprise, isn't. He stole that from Proust, Petra said. There's a famous passage about finding yourself again when you wake in a strange room. It couldn't be in Proust, Gerrit said, when Erasmus would look out all four sides of the tent and say he's seeing a rabbit, a whirl of gnats, a brace of meadowlarks landing and taking off, up down. I slept in the middle, like Petra now, being the neutral element, though Erasmus would reach across and knit fingers with Hansje, and shove and push, by way of some kind of understanding they have. Erasmus was rollicking in our outing because he wasn't, as he said, being hugged and kissed to death. No Toby and Nils rooting and pranking in the bed of a morning. No fights. Just the freedom of the out-of-doors, and friends who were just friends.

• IMPATIENS BIFLORA

The pod has evanescent partitions, with anatropous seeds along a thick axis. Five valves, elastically coiled, spring open when dry, shooting out the seeds.

• 19

Well, Petra said, there was this poster in a shop across from the Centre Pompidou in Paris. A man it showed, with a great body, about twenty, in the buff, holding a baby out in his arms, looking wise and happy, as if it approved of its daddy having an extensive babymaker hanging out and down over tight fat balls, for all the world to see. But behind these fetching two, crossways the poster, were two boys, also britchesless, lying in a hug. Ha, said Gerrit. Anything printed on the poster? Nello asked. No words, Petra said, just the photo.

• 20

Hair muddled, eyelids thick with sleep, Gerrit raised himself on his elbows in the sleeping bag, and said, There's a mist off the river. Whoopee, said Nello, eyes still closed. Petra lay batting her eyes and smiling. Hello, said Gerrit. Don't look, he said, after leaning to give her a kiss, I've got to nip out to pee, and have sprung one. Let's see, said Petra, reaching. No, said Gerrit, blockading with knees. Close your eyes. Petra closed her eyes, looking as soon as Gerrit was out. Wow, she said, straight out and up, and with its hood back. It does that, Nello said, as you know good and well, when the bladder's about to pop. Learn something every day, Petra said, lifting the tent flap and looking out. Gerrit's peeing up. A silver arc, pretty in the mist. Me too, said Nello, scrambling out. Hey, Petra, Nello hollered, it won't go down. Breakfast, said Petra. A fire, water, mush, raisins. I'm impressed. Gerrit, half embarrassed and half pleased with himself, scrounged around in his knapsack until he found briefs, which prodded out in front when he put them on. Bashful, said Petra. Water jug, coffee packets, and come here. I liked kissing all day yesterday. Poor Nello's left out. Don't anybody kiss me, Nello said. As they stood kissing, Petra pushed down Gerrit's briefs, and, squatting, took them off, batting Gerrit's hands away from trying to pull them up again. No clothes we agreed, she said. I'm mortified, said Gerrit.

• LUPINUS CALCARATUS

Erect, high, silky pubescent throughout, leafy. Leaflets 7 to 10, linear lanceolate, acute, mucronate: stipules ovate, acuminate, persistent: flowers in rather close and short raceme, bracts subulate, deciduous, calyx deeply spurred at base, minutely bracteolate, the upper lip short, double-toothed, white, the lower larger, entire, acute: banner and wings somewhat pubescent externally, the keel ciliate: pods hairy, with four seeds. Flowers white, the spur exceeding the pedicels.

• 22

House wren of the Grenadines, said Tumble, mockingbird bananaquit Carib grackle. Buccament, said Quark, Sion Hill Cumberland Questelles

Layou New Ground Mesopotamia Troumaca. Angelfish, said Buckeye, spotfin butterfly. Finite but unbounded, O over under by and through!

• 23

Fainthearted, no, said Petra, but do be fair. Kissing's fun. I'm not looking, Nello said. I'm just here, browning my butt and listening to the meadow, the buzz of it. So what are you doing? Fondling, said Gerrit. Feeling better all the time, said Petra. Everything, anyway, has become unreal. Time has stopped. I think the meadow and river have drifted away from where they were when we came. It's us, Nello said, who are different, and getting differenter all the time. How different will we get? Running around bare-assed is not all that peculiar, and that's not what's doing something to us. We've only each other to say things to: that's a big difference. Last summer Erasmus said all manner of things I'm certain he would never have said back home. We think differently, Petra said, breathing deep after a long kiss. Snuggling on the sunroom couch or at Betje's when she has the house all to herself is always a dare when hands stray to critical places, like now. I'm not looking, Nello said. Why not? Gerrit said. Unfair, Petra said, is unfair, sitting up and monkeying over to Nello, pressing a kiss on the back of his neck. Tickles, he said, after a suspicious silence. But feels good. Does it now! Petra said, neither tease nor mischief in her voice. Gerrit's next. Gerrit's next what? asked Gerrit. Kiss Nello, Petra said. Why ever not?

• SURVEYOR

Gerrit, in his scout shirt because of the morning chill, with Corbusier Homme Modulor shoulder patch, said once they were off the bus at Knollendorp, honest Hans asked Rasmus every tactless question that sprang easily to his liberal mind. In less than ten meters of hiking to the sandspit, he pried into Rasmus's standing as Strodekker's newly adopted son, happy older brother to Nils and Tobias, their involvement with the *Vrijheid* cadres, why he wanted to get away from them for a few days to change the pH factor of his soul, length of his weewee, who his real parents were, if he did it with girls too, how much he got for an allowance, what they did in Denmark and the Federal Republic, why one of his eyes was off-center and jiggled, the length of Strodekker's weewee, and on and on, until Rasmus was shaken inside out but not in the least pissed off. He's as honest as a dog. This is his shirt, from the wild scout troop Strodekker runs. It was when Hansje asked Rasmus if he didn't think that Strodekker's just a mite gaga that I changed the conversation and got a shoulder squeeze of gratitude. What I did was ask Hansje the same questions about his buddy Jan, who was in Italy with his folks, and heard more about him than I really needed to know. So, Petra said, why do you have Erasmus's shirt? He gave it to me, Gerrit said.

• TREES

Four trees upon a solitary acre
Without design
Or order, or apparent action,
Maintain.

The sun upon a morning meets them,
The wind.
No nearer neighbor have they
But God.

The acre gives them place,
They him attention of passerby,
Of shadow, or of squirrel, haply,
Or boy.

What deed is theirs unto the general nature,
What plan
They severally retard or further,
Unknown.

• THREE PERSIMMONS IN A BLUE DISH

Klee Noordzee coast, the sandspit, a Boudin with Cornelius on it, sea blow cocking his hair into a crest of light. Early Mondriaan pine forest with blue shadows, the wood at the top of the meadow. Courbet, the spring. What's more, Gerrit said, is our telescoping aluminum flagpole here on the main brace, flying the Danish flag. For the bunnies, Petra said. They were wondering where we're from. Now they can say, Ah! Lutherans! Dutch flag tomorrow, Gerrit said. Then Swedish, followed by the Norwegian. Today we're Danes.

• 27

The spinney explored, the meadow traversed twice, the sandspit inspected, the rivermouth waded in, they came back to the tent. Bread, cheese, and hot soup, said Petra. We're getting to be the color of gingerbread. And Gerrit's spirited virile member sticks straight out, sort of, rather than toward heaven. Does it feel good? A grin and a blush together are wildly becoming. Cakes and apples, sang Nello, in all the chapels, fine balconies and rich mellow pears. Last summer, Gerrit said, and I'd have been a zoological exhibit, with commentary by Hansje and Rasmus.

• PATROL

Quark on reconnoiter in the wood met Wolf, her gazing eye silver and soot, silent of paw as she strode. Sabina! Quark said in the old Latin, mama of Quirinus, chaster than Vesta, cunninger than Minarva. *Hrff!* said Sabina, *et lactentes ficos et gutulliocae.* Carissa! said Quark. I saw you playing with the frogs and crickets, pretending to dance and pounce, laughing all the while. *Archeotera,* said Sabina, *unde haec sunt omnia nata.* But, said Quark, these are good people, over yonder by the water, the three cubs in a cloth house. They live in a town of canals and lightning run through threads, where they learn, not much, but something, numbers and tongues mainly. I've smelt them, Sabina said, two toms and a bitch, potash and olive, sheep and cottonweed. Metal. Not to do you a mischief, Quark said. The metal is the frame of their house, cups, buckles, and such. It is never prudent to be seen, O Consiliarius. The faith has been gone so long.

• LA CHENILLE ET LA MOUCHE

From the *Jules Verne,* a hot-air balloon hanging unanchored six meters above the meadow, defying both gravity and its own radiant levity, its declinator lever set on *orbit,* hung a rope ladder up which Buckeye, Tumble, and Quark swarmed with the progress of swimming arctic wolves, knees and elbows in the same vertical plane, all three in midshipman's uniforms of the French navy. The propeller turned its four wooden blades idly, like a windmill dreaming. Two brass cylinders leaked steam. The crystal-set telegraph key was chittering patrol signals, asking for reports. Buckeye, standing a bouquet of meadow flowers in the teapot, sat down to the key and sent: *Le travail mène à la richesse.* Ha! said Tumble, that will really interest the dispatcher. *Pauvres poètes, travaillons! Travaillons!* said Quark. *La chenille en peinant sans cesse devient le riche papillon.* Tumble, out of his sailor suit and into plus fours, red flannel shirt, sweater, scarf, aviator cap, goggles, and gauntlets, gave four dials a reading, poking each with a businesslike finger. Ion stream, he said. Neutrinos under however many atmospheres you get from rho over time, divided by the azimuth in hypernewtons. Twenty-three point six eight niner, said Buckeye. Fourier waves in sync. Somebody, Quark said, has been pressing weeds in the log. Now, said Tumble, send them the Fly. Never mind that they're asking for coordinates. That's microswedenborg's point zero zero one by four zero on the nose. The Fly, said Buckeye. *Nos mouches savent des chansons que leur apprirent en Norvège.* Quark, naked between naval togs and flight overall, said of his penis that it was sunburned, along with his behind, and probably his toes and the back of his neck. *Les mouches ganiques qui sont les divinités de la neige.* That ought to hold them until we can achieve drift. We're starting to spin. Rain on white dew, Buckeye recited, all the leaves are yellow. Wait awhile for that, said Quark, and where's the bee balm and cucumber salve for my member and butt, both as red as cherry wine. Look at the late afternoon sun on the inlet down there, Buckeye said, wrinkled quicksilver specked with green and blue. Get those weeds out of the teapot. Let's see it with biscuits and cheese, apples and chocolate. The log, said Quark, who had wrapped himself in a blanket, uncorked the ink bottle, and dipped the quill. Berrying, he wrote. Bees, caterpillars, flies, sycamore polyhedra, three families of field mice, from whom that peculiar joke we still haven't figured out. Gerrit and Petra kissed fifty-four times, or once every ten minutes for nine hours, with Gerrit's piddler going sprack at every kiss.

• QUINCE, AUTUMN RAIN, AND MEDLAR

The Summer Bon Chretien is somewhat a long pear, with a green-and-yellow russetish coat, and sometimes red sides. It is ripe at Michaelmas: some dry them as they do prunes, and keep them all the year after. The Summer Bergamot is an excellent well-relished pear, flat and short, of a mean bigness, and of a dark yellowish green color on the outside. The Primating pear is moist and early ripe. The Russet Catherine is a very good middle-sized pear.

• AND O A GYPSY AIR

From a haversack slung on the taffrail of the nacelle Tumble took a horn, Buckeye a banjo, and Quark a Jew's harp. The balloon was over the spinney, gorgeous and strange. The key of G minor, Tumble said, his hair all whorls and spikes still, as they had an urge in the middle of breakfast (honey, wheat-meal biscuits, and reindeer milk) for music. Where the cacklers, Buckeye said, but no grunters, continuo from Haydn, the tune on the Jew's harp, and I sing. Naked but for a shirt, he attacked the run that began the air with a voice like rung glass and the sweetest of tenor bells. *Where the cacklers, but no grunters shall be set loose for the hunters, those we still must keep alive.* Tumble rocked his shoulders and kept time with his heels as he played the ground, handsomely paced, on the horn. *Aye, and put them forth to thrive in the parks and in the chases, and the finer wallèd places, like Saint Jameses, Greenwich, Tiballs, where the acorns, plump as chiballs, soon shall change both kind and name. Proclaim them then the Kingses game.* Quark broke into a jig, ringing the Jew's harp, and lolling his eyes. *So the act no harm may be unto their keeper Barnabee. It will do as good a service as did ever Gypsy Jarvis.* All instruments down as they sang the last lines trio, in glorious harmony. *Or our Captain Charles, the tall man, and a part too of our salmon!* Golly diddle dingle gunst, said Tumble. Tom Tickler on the tabor, who could bring the girls. Oof. Quark leaned over the rail with the big brass telescope. They're all kissing, time about, he said, and they're having mush and raisins for breakfast.

• BOSNIAN MEADOW MOUSE

They sat in the meadow. Nello said that it could be described botanically, geologically, ecologically, geographically, aesthetically, historically, poetically, but that none of these descriptions would include what they were doing.

• SILENCE, WITH CRICKETS

A throbbing owl call in the night. Talk about spooky, said Nello. Like doves, Petra said, they can swivel their heads all the way around. The little Athenian owl was the *strix*, compact as a jug, mewed from olives, flew sideways, wings as blurred as a hummingbird's. Makes it the cozier, Gerrit said, snuggled here as warm as toast. Admit however, Petra said, that the ground is twice as hard as a floor, and has rocks in it. I'm hungry, Nello said. I'm happy, Gerrit said.

• MASTER JOHN TRADESCANTE'S ORCHARD

The muscadine, some call the Queen Mother plum, and some the Cherry Plum, is fair and red, of a reasonable bigness and ripe about Bartholmy Tide. The Flushing Bullace grows in a thick cluster like grapes. The Morocco plum is black like a Damson, well tasted, and somewhat dry in eating. The Green Peasecod plum is long and pointed, and ripe in the beginning of September. The Amber plum is round and as yellow as wax, coming clean from the stone like an apricock. The Red Mirobalane plum grows to be a great tree quickly, spreading thick and far, like the Black Thorn or Sloe.

• THE SCENERY IS ROMANTIC IF IT HAS STEPS

There's a gerbil in the telephone, Quark said, eating goober peas. Give it a thump, said Buckeye. Josephine Geronimo and Virgilia Tardy were present at the planting of poplars in the marshes. The toms are coming from the spring in the grove, carrying a bucket of water between them, free arms out for balance and leverage. The one with thick dark hair that makes jug handles over his ears still has a stiff jubilator. It flops and bounces as he walks. The other, with hair the color of ripe wheat, is singing *Der Vogelfänger bin ich ja*. The *virguncula* is outside the tent pouring heated water into tin cups already containing dehydrated essence of cow milk, van Houten's powdered cocoa, and refined Jamaican sugar. She presses her lips against the lips of each of the toms when they bring her the water. Meanwhile, the family of rabbits in the spinney is out in the sun, nibbling. Buckeye, having made some persnickety adjustments to the rigging, touched a drop of oil to the propeller shaft and advanced the roller map a smitch, began a little quickstep dance, snapping his fingers, singing softly but briskly, as if under his breath, in Faeroese. Tumble, climbing aboard up the rope ladder, swung a jeaned leg over the taffrail, wrecked Quark's hair because he was on the telephone, and joined Buckeye's dance, nose to nose, knee to knee. Say what? Quark shouted into the telephone. I have maniacs on board, unbuttoning each other's clothes. Yes, Buck and Tumble, to be sure. There's no other patrol in this sector closer than a star circle, is there? Didn't think so. Ariel by Hizqiyya! Over. Out.

• 3 6

Two kinds of ants, red and black. They probably have wars. And some of the mice have little white pants and some are cinnamon gray and make round nests on stalks. We'll never get all the bugs identified. Gnats are the neutrinos of the place. Meadow birds and river birds. Highland grass, lowland grass: it's the sandspit and the river that accounts for that. Time to kiss. Yuck, said Nello, but if that's the game. Long hug, long kiss, Petra said, two full minutes, and see if Nello's wizzle bobs its head again, and after three butting throbs stands bolt upright. Bobtail dominicker, Gerrit counted, little poll ram. Three zoll, four zoll, zickerzoll bam! Poker up on four. Don't open your eyes, Nello niddy, and you won't get the giggles. And your blushes turn your tan purple. Nello likes being kissed, likes kissing. You're over two minutes. Better make it last, Cornelius Bezemsteel, as I'm next, and on the mouth this time.

• THE CAT'S WIFE HAS WHISKERS TOO

Jam, said Tumble, strawberry jam. I think I got the clothes wrong, though. Cassock, or smock, belted over linsey-woolsey trews, and hook-and-eye boots, are not period, and the old woman who sold me the jam was still looking at the money when I left. I think Wardrobe and Props tease us. Jam

on Ryvitas, however, is good stuff, yuss? It will give us a bellyache if we eat
the whole jar. Rabbit, Quark said, showed me some sweetgrass today, a nice
fresh taste with a tang of ginger in it. She said it was excellent as a digestive.

• L'ACOUSTIQUE PAYSAGISTE

What, Gerrit said, if you knew everything. All music, all painting, all writing, had met everybody, and been everywhere. You'd be crazy, Petra said,
humming more of the First Brandenburg Concerto that Gerrit had been
whistling to an imaginary viola. That's not what knowing's about. Of course
you have to know enough to begin to discriminate, but from there on out
it's pick and choose. Besides, everything's not for everybody. There's tem-
perament, and talent, and disposition.

• 39

The life! Nello said, roughing it, camping in a meadow, going bare-bot-
tomed, grub all flavored with ashes, crick in the neck and back from sleeping
on the ground. Chocolate bars, though wrecked in transit, Petra said, are not
flavored with wood ash. Clover, bees, sorrel, knotgrass, ants, partridges
(*juck* is what they say, said Gerrit, if we were to see one, never mind hearing
one), owls (heard, but not yet seen), gnats. But, said Nello, I absoposifuck-
inglutetively will not kiss Gerrit. Why not? Petra asked. Yes, said Gerrit,
why not?

• ANTONIO GRAMSCI IN PRISON

Milky blue at the horizon, the sky prospered toward a rich and solid azure
overhead. Gerrit, a bandana around his forehead, its knot ducktailed out
from his nape, stood at attention, pectorals squeezed in tight and flat, butt
hard, hands flat on thighs, shoulders squared, the tucked corners of his
mouth wry, fighting off hilarity, toes wiggling, tongue in cheek, eyes merry.
Nothing, Petra said, think of absolutely nothing. White mind. They'll pay
me to tell this, Cornelius said. It's worth trying, Petra said, if you want it to
go down. I feel like a sexpot with red pouting lips and a raccoon ring of
mascara around my eyes, steamy at the crotch, rather than the stickstraight
begoggled plain Socialist brainy wonder that I am. This is what happens
when you're the only girl around. Hormones in well-behaved boys know

I'm here, nip down to your gonads with chemical messages to trigger sper-matogenesis, which has given you satyriasis. Feels good, said Gerrit. You don't think our kissing for days and days has had anything to do with it? Oh no, said Cornelius, nor the rest of it. Now I'm getting one again.

• WITTGENSTEIN ON A CAISSON

Humming Beethoven. The sky rotten with a bilge drift of clouds like squid ink coiling in milk. Lice in the seams of tunic and trousers. A red fungus burning between his toes. Death is not an event in life.

• 42

Mullein must have room enough to spread its fine rosette of basal leaves if it is to erect its Jacob's staff. It cannot be crowded even by grass. It is a bien-nial, and cannot establish itself in cultivated fields. It is found in meadows and pastures and along fences that are not too much overgrown.

• MEADOW

Aujourd'hui comme aux temps de Pline et de Columelle la jacinthe se plaît dans les Gaules, la pervenche en Illyrie, la marguerite sur les ruines de Nu-mance et pendant qu'autour d'elles les villes ont changé de maîtres et de noms, que plusiers sont entrées dans le néant, que les civilizations se sont choquées et brisées, leurs paisibles générations ont traversé les âges et sont arrivées jusqu'à nous, fraîches et riantes comme aux jours des batailles.

• TWO ACORNS, ONE GINGKO LEAF

The great things, Gerrit said, hair windsprung and sunny, a rust of sunburn across his nose, are how to get rid of wars, bombs, bankers, prejudice, hun-ger, meanness, and who was Jesus. When you two are kissing, Cornelius said, at least Gerrit can't talk. He purrs, Petra said. Erasmus, Gerrit said, woke one morning with an erection hard as a broomstick, complete with balls scrunched up tight, like mine. Like ours, Cornelius said. Hansje was all for hanky-panky, but Erasmus put a damper on that. Poor Hansje, Petra said. But I'm glad there's somebody who can say what he can't do. We climbed practically all the trees in the spinney, explored the other spit over the hill there, swam, and generally mucked about, seriously silly, with forays into all those intellectual things Erasmus and Hansje can carry on for days, like making endless lists out of their heads, history and science and films, with Hansje sneaking in the odd naughty bit. So like late in the afternoon, Erasmus said that if he whacked off he'd keep from gunking up the sleeping bag that night, and started in, offhandedly dextrous, so to speak, except that he's a lefthander. Offhandedly, Petra said. While walking around and talking, gathering sticks for the fire. Hansje's eyes were a study. Big and round, as if he had more schemes than he could deal with, and needed to hit on the right one first crack out of the box. Erasmus can laugh with his eyes better than anybody, also read minds. So he started this long talk about sheepwalks and Roman roads, and every once in a while he'd close his eyes because his wizzle was feeling so good, and slow his stroke, and gasp. All this to hypnotize Hansje, who was being cool like crazy, fighting off paying the least attention, because those were the rules of the game. Explain it, Petra said, reaching over to give Gerrit's balls a squeeze. Watch it, he said. Why? said Petra. Rules of the game, said Gerrit. In your story or right now? Cornelius asked. Both, said Petra. I want to hear why. It just was, Gerrit said. We had agreed to prove that we're the masters of our bodies, and not them of us, I'm quoting Erasmus, who gets all this day in and day out from his composite family, which sometimes seems to be a Roman bathhouse in the last five minutes of the empire, and sometimes a Montessori kindergarten devoted to ethics and hygiene. Suntans of ultimate golden brown, fresh air, exercise, fellowship, life tough and simple, radical sweet innocence: Erasmus kept saying all this, and Hansje and I ate it all in, so that when he himself said he was slaking animal lust that was a natural function of the organism, how could Hansje and I be transparent copycats? Golly, Petra said, the things I don't know about. Nello, are you understanding this? Sure, said Cornelius, every word. I can finish the story. Erasmus was being a devil lording it over two innocents, for the fun of watching them squirm. You think? Gerrit asked. He said that it was the longest he'd gone without coming in years, and that it was a big thing for him to be in the sleeping bag with us as friends only, and to be barebutt with us all day. Confusing, said Petra, but only a bit strange, you know? Do I? Gerrit asked. I mean, know? Sure, Petra said. So finish the story. Ha, said Gerrit. When Hansje was about to fizz over and invite us all to join him in an orgy, Erasmus quit, shrugged his shoulders, and said maybe he didn't need to, after all. He really is a devil, Petra said. How long did it take him to drive Hansje and you crazy?

• 45

Quark on the telephone in the nacelle of the balloon. Yuss, he said, I know, but I'm more interested in a nest of crystals we found back of the spring in the spinney. The series is in fifths of a rotation, optimal foci of tetrahedra on a very long axis. What? I'm putting Buckeye on the thread. Here he is. Ho! said Buckeye, it's lovely. They're asleep now, in a heap, arms and legs every which way. I was too shy to look. Here's Tumble, whose imagination it all rather caught. Hello hello, said Tumble. Well, nothing that would get into a poem by Catullus, but then they weren't arctic hares up on their hind legs batting at each other, either. Actually they're not in a heap, as Buck said. They're up and have the lantern lit in the tent, and have broken out biscuits and made cocoa, and are laughing and kissing all around. Sabina the wolf is scandalized, and the owl in the sycamore has offered comments also. Band two alpha for that, Ariel by Hizqiyya. They're talking about hot chocolate in a café in Amsterdam on a cold day, with sleet, Édouard Manet, Bishop Desmond Tutu, Petra's mother's fanatic housekeeping, the legs of Joaquin Carvalho Cruz, the failure of Danes to understand any joke whatsoever, bicycles, Mondriaan's admiration of Mae West, Queen Wilhelmina's battiness, Daley Thompson, Wittgenstein's chocolate oatmeal, Erasmus Strodekker's off eye and membrum virile, Mary Lou Retton, the boulevards of Paris, gosling motilities among the precocious, Petra's breasts by lantern light, the best ways to ripen pears, Gerrit's foreskin, the coziness of the tent, friendship's liberation from reticence, owls, zebras, Mozart, the quiet of the meadow in the middle of the night, why it was nobody's business if Gerrit kissed Nello, or Nello Petra, tennis racquets, the clarity of the stars seen through the tent flaps, how wide awake they were, and eyes blue with fate.

Pyrrhon of Elis

Four years before the birth of Alexandros of Makedonia, Pyrrhon the Skeptic Philosopher was born in Elis, a country town in the northwest of the Peloponnese known throughout the civilized world as the site of the Olympic Games. He was trained as a painter. For some years you could see a mural of his in one of the gymnasia, runners carrying torches. He was educated by Stilpon or Bruson, or by Stilpon's son Bruson: the life that has come down to us of Pyrrhon is a copy made by a scribe ignorant of Greek.

He rounded out his education by travelling with Anaxarkhos to India, where he studied with the naked sophists, and to Persia, where he learned from the Magi. He returned to Elis an agnostic who withheld his opinion of every matter. He denied that anything was good or bad, right or wrong. He doubted that anything exists, said that habits and custom dictate our actions, and would not allow that a thing is either more this than that on its own.

He thus went out of his way for nothing, leaving all to chance, and was wholly incautious with encounters, whether with carts in the street, cliffs toward which he was walking, or dogs. He said he had no reason to believe that his solicitude for his welfare was wiser than the results of an accident. Antigonos of Karystos tells us that his friends followed him about to keep him from falling into rivers, wells, and ditches. He lived for ninety years.

He lived apart from the world, having been taught in India that no man could teach the good who was at the beck and call of a patron, or had to toady to a king. He avoided even his relatives.

He kept his composure at all times. If all of the audience drifted away while he was lecturing, he finished the lecture just as if there were people listening. He liked to fall into conversation with strangers and go with them wherever they were going. For days at a time, none of his pupils or friends knew where he was.

Once, when his master Anaxarkhos had fallen into a ditch full of mud up to his neck and could not get out, Pyrrhon chanced to pass by. He noticed Anaxarkhos but paid him no heed. He was much censured by the unenlightened for this indifference, but Anaxarkhos praised his disciplined apathy and courageous suppression of affection.

He often talked to himself. When questioned about this, he replied that he was teaching himself how to be good. He was a formidable debater, sharp at cross-examination and skilled in logic. The philosopher Epikouros, an admirer from a distance, was always curious to know the latest doings and sayings of Pyrrhon. As for the Eleans, they were so proud of Pyrrhon that they elected him *arkhiereos* for festivals and sacrifices, and remitted his, and all other philosophers', taxes.

He was made an honorary citizen of Athens. He lived with his sister, who was a midwife. He was not above taking produce to market, and could be seen at the stalls selling poultry, garlic, and honey. He was known to dust the house and sweep the floors for his sister, and was once seen washing the pig.

Once he came to his sister Philista's defense in an argument among the neighbors. This seemed inconsistent with his doctrine of apathy, no matter what the disturbance, but he replied that a noble mind always came to the defense of a helpless woman. And once, when he showed alarm at a dog that was biting him on the leg, he replied that it is impossible to refine away all human responses to the world.

His great teaching was that we should resist reality with all our might, denying it in actions where possible, with words, where not.

It is told that when he had an abscess that had to be treated with stinging ointments, and eventually cauterized with a white-hot poker, he neither winced nor frowned.

Philon the Athenian, a friend, records that of thinkers he was most admiring of Demokritos the Atomist, and that his favorite line of poetry was Homer's

As are the generations of leaves so are the generations of men.

He approved of Homer's comparing men to wasps, flies, and birds. When a storm came up, and the ship in which he was making a voyage was in danger, all the passengers were terrified except Pyrrhon, who pointed to a sow in a crate, calmly eating. He once dismissed a student who flew into a fury and chased the cook into the street with his spit, the roast still on it. As he would never tell his students what he was thinking, or answer a question, they were always in a quandary, and never knew what they were supposed to know. He said he was like Homer in holding different opinions at different times. He approved of the sayings

Nothing too much.
A promise is a curse standing at your elbow.

He liked the poetry of Arkhilokhos, because it emphasizes our being at the mercy of God and the tragic brevity of life. His heritage includes Euripides' pessimism, Xenophanes' agnosticism, Zeno's denial of motion, and Demokritos' dismissal of the witness of the senses to reality. His followers agree with Demokritos that we know nothing, for truth is down a well.

His pupils were taught to doubt and deny everything, even that they were doubting and denying everything. *Not more so than not!* they replied to all, even that honey is sweeter than grapes, or that virtue is less harmful than vice. There is nothing true that is not probably as untrue as it is true.

Of perplexities arising from the teachings of Pyrrhon there are ten, and here is the way out of each of them:

I. That there are things useful or harmful to our lives. But every creature finds different things harmful or useful. The quail fattens on hemlock, which is deadly to man.

II. That nature is a continuum through all creatures. But Demophon, the butler to Alexandros the Great, warmed himself in the shade and shook with cold in the sun. Aristotle tells us that Andron of Argos crossed the Libyan desert without water.

III. That perception is whole. But we see the yellow of an apple, smell its fragrance, taste its sweetness, feel its smoothness, hold its weight.

IV. That life is even and the world always the same. But the world of a sick man is a different one from that of the hale man. We are different of mind asleep than when awake. Joy and grief change everything for us. The young man moves in a world different from that of the old. Courage knows a road that timidity cannot guess. The hungry see a world unknown to the fed. Perikles had a slave who walked on the rooftop in his sleep never falling off. In what world live the mad, the stingy, the spiteful?

V. That there is a reality beyond custom, law, religion, and philosophy. But each set of beliefs and attitudes regards the same innocent things with widely differing eyes. A Persian can with propriety marry his daughter, the Greek considers this a crime without equal. The Massagetai have their own women in common. The Egyptians preserve their dead in spices and tar, the Romans burn theirs, the Greeks bury theirs.

VI. That things have identities in themselves. But everything varies from context to context. Purple is a different color near red than near green, in a room or in full sunlight. A rock is lighter in water than out of it. And most things are mixtures, the components of which we would not recognize in themselves.

VII. That objects in space are evident as to position and distance. But the sun, large enough a fire to warm all the earth, is small because of its distance. A circle seen at an angle seems to be oval, on end, a line. Harsh, gray mountains seem from far away to be blue and smooth. The just risen moon is much larger than the moon high in the sky, yet its size has not changed. A fox in a brake looks quite different from a fox in a field. Who can decide what's the shape of a dove's neck? Everything is known as a figure in a ground, or not at all.

VIII. That quantity and quality have knowable properties. But a little wine strengthens, a lot weakens. Swiftness is relative to other speeds. Heat and cold are known only by comparison.

IX. That there are strange and rare things. But earthquakes are common in parts of the world, rain rare in others.

X. That relations among things can be stated. But right to left, before and behind, up and down, depend on infinite variables, and it is the nature of the world that everything is always changing about. A brother to a sister is not the same relation as a brother to a brother. What is a day? So many hours? So much sunlight? The time between midnights?

Agrippa says that these perplexities can be reduced to five. Reality will always admit of disagreement among its observers. As every proposition can serve as the basis for another, you can never complete a picture of reality. A thing can be known in relation to something else, therefore nothing can be known in itself. All hypotheses must be built up from basic particulars which we must take for granted, but to take them for granted is not thinking but supposing. To confirm one thing by another, as we always must, is to move in a futile circle.

Demonstration is therefore impossible, as are certainty, significance, cause, motion, knowing, becoming, and evaluation. Pyrrhon wrote nothing, but his disciples Timon, Ainesidemos, Noumenios, and Nausiphanes have left us many scrolls discussing the hopelessness of knowing anything at all, or of having any certainty that we or anything else exists, or can exist. Assailed by logic and by realists, they have all admitted that they are by no means certain of their uncertainty. We will admit apparent fact, they say, but will not admit that what we think we seem to see is what it actually is. We see that fire burns, or seems to, but cannot go beyond that to say that all fire burns, or that God intended fire to burn. Honey has, on the limited occasions we have tasted it, been sweet, but whether it is sweet we do not know. We certainly do not know if it is the nature of honey to be sweet, or if it is sweet to other tongues.

So for ninety years Pyrrhon, the son of Pleistarkhos, lived (except for his travels to India and Persia) in the charming town of Elis, with its horse-breeding citizens; and Olympic coaches and umpires; its swarm of splendid athletes and spectators every four years; its shady streets with sleeping hogs and their nursing litters; yellow dogs running in packs; choruses of Spartan trumpeters; fleets of Corinthian girl companions with raccoon eyes, pink frills, and Asiatic embroidery from shoulder to heel and gaits as if to the flutes of Lydia; goats in a mist of flies; eloquent sculptors talking style in the wine-shops; long-haired painters jibbering over onion stew in the ordinaries; mathematicians playing chess under the chinaberry trees; children tossing knucklebones in the parks under the gaze of Gorgon nannies; ladies of the Sodality of Hera rolling through the avenues in donkey carts, demure under parasols; grizzled philosophers and their raunchy boyfriends tumbling naked in the palaistra as recreation from the Pythagorean numbers and the metaphysics of Aristoteles (which had a brief vogue during the Alexandrian Epoch); garlicky Italians studying virtue and manners under the sophists; rich Lakedaimonian military strategists who wore undyed and goatish smocks and lived off porridge and river water; potters; farmers; cabinet makers; poultry dealers; saddlers; hostlers; poets; cooks; musicians; the Little Bears of Artemis dancing *The Elean Shoe* and *The Solstice Hop* under the strict eye of a priestess; little boys with hair like mops playing hopscotch in the magistrate's yard; pious blacksmiths; Roman lawyers and their fat wives; sportswriters who concocted epigrams for Olympic victors' statues; a sad Gaul who was writing a book about the moon; acrobats; priests of every mystery you could think of, Eleusinian, Delian, Sabazian, Dodonian, what have you, even a brown Egyptian who ran a temple of Isis and Osiris down near the tanning yard (much heckled by the stable boys); in short, a fine round world of people and things, seasons and years and rumors of other worlds as far away as the Indus and the Nile, the Thames forever hidden by fog and the Danube said to be as blue as a Doric eye; but was honestly uncertain that he did, and would never admit to any of it.

We Often Think of Lenin at the Clothespin Factory

A city, not Paris. NOTCH, *an old woman in a chair made from a barrel, beside a tall porcelain stove, a basket of potatoes in her lap. Kerchief, shawl, ample skirts, boots.* POLDEN, *a young soldier with lots of brown curly hair, Mongol cheekbones, green uniform with scarlet shoulder tabs.*

NOTCH

There was once an Englishman named Vernon.
He was hunting hyenas near Carthage.
This was back in the nineteenth century.
He stumbled and fell into an abyss.
He was surprised, however, going down,
That it seemed indeed to have no bottom
And when one came, it was as if he'd dropped
Down into a great goosefeather mattress.
What's more, he was coming back up again,
Rising on a steady and busy heave
Which by degrees brought him to the pit's edge
And rolled him out onto *terra firma*.
He had fallen into a mass of bats
Which, disturbed from their slumber, had risen

All together out of the deep abyss
And brought the English hunter up with them.

POLDEN

Is that true?

NOTCH

Every beautiful word.

My husband Osip read it in a book.
He was a poet. They took him away.
I have all of his poems off by heart.

POLDEN

Are they published in a book?

NOTCH

No, never.

One of them is about the Old Cockroach
Seeing his face in the shine of his boots.

POLDEN

Did he write a poem about Lenin
Taking a walk in his automobile?

NOTCH

The square. Barracks of the Guard to the north.
Flagpole with flag. Blue sentries pacing there,
Scarlet facings with the odd number nine
In gold threadwork on their tunic collars.
They pace, cold, along the top of the wall,
Pace from the turrets to the tower gate
Where they meet, and about-face with a stomp,
And then tread back to the turrets again.
Below, along the blank wall, another
Pair of cold guards make the same cold movements.

POLDEN

The square, west. Friedrich Engels Institute.
Iron doors. Allegory of Labor.
Classical columns. Red bunting banners
Across the front on anniversaries.
Sometimes, a delegation with roses
From the People's Republic of China.
The committee from Shqiperija
No longer visits, nor its football team.
The windows are lit at night twice a year
And then you can hear Rimsky-Korsakov.

NOTCH

But not Stravinsky or Francis Poulenc.
The square, south. The Ministry of Culture.
Bicyclists from Czechoslovakia.
Paintings by Aleksandr Deineka.
Sevastopol Dynamo Aquasports
Workers' Summer Vacation Swimming Pool.
And *Lenin Taking a Walk in His Car.*

POLDEN

Peasant embroidery from Hungary.
Lenin teaching history to children.

NOTCH

The square, east. Ministry of Peace. The Dom.
Though it is understood that modern men
Do not light candles in Sankt Pavl's Dom,
They still wear garlic against the Devil
And say nine novenas under their breath
When they have heard an owl hoot at night
Or by evil luck a bootlace has snapped
Or the mirror has fallen from the wall.

Women and children slip into the Dom
Before they have to go and wait in lines.

POLDEN

Old women do talk.

NOTCH

Puppies make doodoo.
Another tale, already. Herr Schriftbild,
A publisher, as soon as he had found
The apartment building specified in
Robert Walser a Swiss writer's letter,
In a court off a square, both with children
And dogs, also found Walser's door inside,
And, drawing the pull, heard a bell jangle
On a bouncing coil of wire deep within.
An interval, and the door was opened
By a butler in a swallowtail coat.

POLDEN

Capitalism.

NOTCH

With large liquid eyes,
Military moustache, hair brushed back
With such parallel regularity
That you suspected a pigtail in back.

POLDEN

Imperialism, English navy.

NOTCH

Was this, Herr Schriftbild asked, the apartment
Where Herr Robert Walser the writer lived?

Exactly, Sir, said the butler, taking
Herr Schriftbild's card.

POLDEN

Decadent plutocrats.

NOTCH

If the Herr Schriftbild would wait a moment,
Herr Walser would be told of his presence,
Which, in very fact, he was expecting.

POLDEN

What a prick.

NOTCH

Herr Schriftbild sat. He took in,
By way of passing the time, the carpet,
Old furniture, strange pictures on the walls,
Probably German, certainly modern,
Some meadow flowers in a blue pitcher,
A paper parrot on a bamboo perch,
A chromolithograph of Palmyra,
A plaster bust of Gottfried von Leibniz,
One of whose eyes had been outlined in red.
A blank brick wall, the view from the window.
Clearly, he thought, it pleases this Walser
To let visitors cool their heels awhile.
Perhaps he was ending a paragraph,
Seeing another visitor, female,
Down the back stairs? Then again, you never
Knew what these writers might not be doing.
Paring their toenails, sitting in a trance,
Reading right through the French dictionary.
And this one, now, could afford a butler.

POLDEN

A pampered bourgeois.

NOTCH

The carpet had lived
At many addresses before this one,
The chairs had ridden through the streets in carts
Pulled by elderly horses. Herr Schriftbild
Avoided the paper parrot's yellow
And Leibniz's red eye and gazed instead
At the flyspecked ruins of Palmyra,
And was wondering if that city is
In the Bible or profane history
When the door through which the butler had gone
Opened just enough to admit a man
In rumpled corduroy and blue flannel
Shirt as fancied by British Socialists.
Large liquid eyes, military moustache.
If his bohemian hair were brushed back
With a parallel regularity,
You would suspect a pigtail tied behind.

POLDEN

Imperialism, English navy.

NOTCH

God help us, Herr Schriftbild said to himself,
This is the butler wanting me to think
He's Walser, who has some frump on his lap,
Or is reading the French dictionary.
The voice, however, greeting Schriftbild
With a familiar and bright nonchalance,
Was wholly different from the butler's.

POLDEN

Karl Marx brooding with folded arms, his head
Massive in bronze, Lenin raising his fist,
Exhorting the people.

NOTCH

Walser, you see,
Was his own butler. He could do voices.
A poet. After a while, he gave up
And lived in a lunatic asylum.
Our poets all went into prisons.

POLDEN

His own butler?

NOTCH

The world was like that, then.
Variety. Versatility. O!
The century before ours, the nineteenth,
It was a kind of earthly paradise.
Avenues of lindens and of poplars.
Men, women, and children, horses and dogs.
And now it's only old women sweeping.
News of tomatoes at a market
Over near Tramstop 6 on the Prospekt.
As soon, ha! believe the clowns at the Cyrk.
They would be gone, anyway, when you came.

POLDEN

In America gangs roam the cities,
Taking the workers' money at knife point.
The rich, without conscience or character,
Are addicted to narcotics and die
Drunk in hideous automobile wrecks.
Imagine fifty thousand wrecks a year.

The sole policy of the government
Is to suppress freedom and to finance
Fascism all over the world.

NOTCH
Heigh ho.

POLDEN
At Sankt Boris some poets and workers
Staged a protest last Tuesday in the street.
They had a 1917 banner
And some modern paintings done on cardboard.
The Ideal of Life they called one of them
And *What Does It All Mean?* was the other.
Very ugly, the paintings. Daubs, in fact.
One of the poets was wearing blue jeans
Made in Pinsk, hammer-and-sickle label.
They did not fit and did not have the look
Of Western jeans, and the blue was purple.
The poet shouted a pukey poem
Before the Guard came and took them away.

NOTCH
The Old Cockroach.

POLDEN
And the gypsies are back.
They have made a camp where the synagogue
Used to be. With beautiful white horses.
Why was he his own butler?

NOTCH
For the joke.
People used to do such things. It was fun.

POLDEN

Silver thunder. That was in the poem.

NOTCH

A bust of Pomona, and a cabbage.
A copy of *The Red Dawn* beside her.
The goods train, when it passed, rattled the cups
And made Pomona shake. The window shook.
And a shiver of light opened her eyes.
That was long ago. In old poetry
She is the spirit of apples and pears,
A tall woman dressed in flowers and leaves.
The clock on the tower no longer works.
Still, it is a fragment of Italy
Here in the gray, in the sameness, the drab.

POLDEN

You live in the past.

NOTCH

I live in my mind.

POLDEN

Her mind.

NOTCH

Where dreams appear in old colors.
Come, shadow, come, and take this shadow up,
Scarlet in the shadow of an orange.
Words.
This oak, this owl, this moon.
There is a
Death in this wind the owl cannot find.
Death in the thistle, white loaf of the moon,
Death in snow, the cricket and wildflowers.

You do not know, Polden Wolf Eyes, what things
There used to be. The thousand-branched oak tree,
With a thousand leaves a branch, red red leaves,
The red oak of Velimir Khlebnikov.
That was red.
                    Now there are no more cities,
Only distances of stone. Verona
Was yellow, Venice was red. And we had
Urbs et fanum, city and cathedral,
Gorod i khram, and bell sound in the air.
Being's the gift. It's difficult to be.

                              POLDEN

But I am, and you are. What is so hard?

                              NOTCH

The stitch of things. He had a mind that was
Part centaur and part streets of Megara.
That was a lecture I once heard in school,
About Theognis, ancient Greek poet.
Silver-rooted waters of Tartessos!
You wouldn't know. He wrote of oiled athletes,
Laws of property, and of irony
And rhythm in behavior, of archers,
Real wealth and vain wealth, loving friends, good talk.
He was critical of democracy,
Muttering that horses were better bred
Than sons and daughters. He fancied the studs
Of both genera, a wide-minded man.

                              POLDEN

That's against nature.

NOTCH

Lenin was a prig.
Theognis lived through a revolution
That cost him his books, olive groves and house,
His racehorses.

POLDEN

Good.

NOTCH

And another war
That cost him his Spartan control of self.
He moved from city to city, always Greek,
Writing in a geometry of words
A poem that was to Homer's beauty
And the verve of Hesiod what later
Apollos modelled on gymnastic slaves
Were to the stiff archaic *kouroi*.

POLDEN

You remember all this?

NOTCH

Shakespeare and Petrarch.
It keeps coming back. Lensky and Pushkin.
Willows and stars.

POLDEN

Before the *Aurora*
Flew the red flag. A moment of glory.

NOTCH

There is a woman sweeping the crossing.
You see her: over there.

POLDEN
I see her, yes.

NOTCH
The clock tower and the barracks. Do you
See how they make a perspective for her,
As in a painting by Canaletto?

POLDEN
Italian landscapist. Hermitage.

NOTCH
And the sky above her, dull as a ditch.
What is she thinking of?

POLDEN
Nothing. Lenin.

NOTCH
Save the hectic red, the bilious yellow
Of the flag over the barracks, there is
No color anywhere.

POLDEN
None. Patch of red,
Smitch of yellow. All of the rest is gray.
You are going to make something of it,
As if she could help being a figure
Alone in the square. She is a picture
In your imagination.

NOTCH
Old woman
Is what she is. Events happen again
In memory, knowing, or narrative.

Time rolls up as it goes along, bringing
The past with it. Nothing is left behind.

POLDEN

That old woman with the besom gets paid
Ahead of the commissars in the line.

NOTCH

Rilke and Lou Andreas Salome
Visited at Yasnaya Polyana.
They talked about Harriet Beecher Stowe.
Ah! the music, string quartets. Poetry.
You could meet someone who had seen Monet
At Giverny, beside the lily pond.
Proust. If you knocked on his door his servant
Had the same set speech for everybody:
Monsieur Proust wants you to know that there is
No waking hour when he is not thinking
Of you, but right now he is too busy
To see visitors. The Boratinskies,
Khlebnikov, Tatlin, Osip Mandelstam.
People who had been to Gertrude Stein's house.
Who recommended that you come? was what
She asked at the door. What a time that was,
Back then.

POLDEN

        Parasites.

NOTCH

            Venice, Rome, London.
Every shop had potatoes for sale,
Heaps and hampers of potatoes for sale.
Oranges, grapes, editions of Homer.
And Lenin had the cleanest bicycle

In Zürich. And he did Indian clubs.
One two three, one two three. At the window.

> POLDEN

If there had been no Lenin, there would have
Been a Lenin.

> NOTCH

And a sealed German train.
Red flags on the locomotive, a crowd
To welcome him at the Finland Station.
Committee of peasants wanting to learn
Hegelian dialectic.

> POLDEN

A workers' brass
Band playing the Internationale.

> NOTCH

Springtimes were sweeter, summers were greener.
The apple trees, the singing, and the gold.
There is no kindness now in the years.

> POLDEN

But there are years.

> NOTCH

Oh yes, the promised years,
Right on time.

Bronze Leaves and Red

He sleeps on an iron cot and his only income is the royalty the State pays him for the use of his portrait on our postage stamps. They say he can sit by the hour regarding a bust of Nietzsche. He likes to chat with his friends on the telephone. The sole decoration he wears is his Iron Cross. That and the armband of the Party are the only accents that alleviate the drab plainness of his uniform. His favorite composer is Anton Bruckner, the strong surge and harmonic progressions of whose symphonies remind him of the old Germany, the forests and the mountains, the coffeehouses with their newspapers, chess games, metaphysical conversations, and scientific journals, the Germany of fine autumns and mists when between the hamlets the little roads are lined with trees whose bronze leaves and red burn with a kind of glory in the afternoon sun.

He has one afternoon visited both the widow of Wagner and Nietzsche's sister. He was often stopped on the way by villagers anxious to admire him. They know that he has a sweet tooth for macaroons and present him with platters of them. He jokes that he will lose his figure, he who is so spare and lean. Nevertheless, he accepts and chews a macaroon, and old women clasp their hands and press them to their cheeks. He is especially fond of children. His eyes light up at the sight of a little blond girl with blue eyes.

With Wagner's widow he discussed the Ring, with Nietzsche's sister the political question of the Jews. He asks to see the philosopher's writing table, his primitive typewriter, his duelling sword from student days, his Italian cape. He is shown the philosopher's teacup, and with a congenial deference he explains that he does not drink tea or coffee, or smoke, or imbibe alcohol except for the occasional stoup of beer in the company of fellow Party members.

His life is austere. It is said by some that in a beautiful actress he has a bosom friend whose gay laughter and pleasant ways beguile him from the cares of the State after a day of reviewing Bavarian labor battalions, of meeting with diplomats, generals, and architects, of inspecting armaments, model communities, and barracks.

He knows everything. His study of Bolshevism, state finance, defense, racial purity, destiny, the German soul, music, city planning, military history, and nutrition has been profound.

He speaks German only. We all find it charming that the only alien word he knows is the English word *gentleman*. He respects learning in others. Not since Frederick the Great have we had so intellectual a leader. He admires Mussolini his gift of languages, his literary talent, his organizational genius, his classical flair for triumphal parades and ancient Roman dignity.

His sense of humor is delicious. Once, out driving in his Mercedes, wearing an aviator cap to keep his hair in place, he exceeded the speed limit by a few miles only and was haled to the shoulder by a motorcycle policeman.

— Follow me, the policeman said, to the Magistrate's in the next township, where you will catch it.

— Follow him, he instructed his chauffeur corporal.

The policeman, you see, did not recognize who was in the Mercedes, because of the aviator cap, but the guard at the Magistrate's saw who was entering the building, and gave a salute, and the Magistrate gave a salute, and everyone froze.

— I have been arrested for speeding, he said to the Magistrate, who opened his mouth like a fish, struck dumb. When capable of it, the Magistrate whispered a word that sounded like *mistake*.

— Not a bit of it, he said. We were well over the limit, and whereas I was not heeding the speedometer, I will not blame my chauffeur corporal but take full responsibility myself, like a proper citizen. Germans are law-abiding folk, are we not?

— Yes! all cried.

— Sieg! he shouted.

— Heil! they all replied.

And he paid the fine. On the way back to his car he was stopped by a little girl with blond hair and blue eyes who gave him a macaroon from a saucer. He ate it, and picked her up and kissed her. Her mother and all the towns-people were watching in an ecstasy. He waved to them as he drove away, back to Berlin and the pitiless responsibilities of his office.

He is a connoisseur of the fine arts and has frequently astounded the professors of aesthetics. He is fond of paintings of weeping clowns, a subject he maintains that Rembrandt would excel in were Rembrandt with us today. He collects still lifes of beer steins and grapes with must on the cluster, conversation pieces depicting a family at table. He is not taken in by the cynical scrawls of inverts so fashionable during the postwar depression. He knows drawing when he sees it, and color, and proportion. It is a charming characteristic of his Viennese taste that he has a weakness for light opera and for films with a romantic theme.

His speeches are electrifying. His command of minutiae keeps the engineers and tacticians on their toes. Manufacturers and bankers come away from his conferences gasping at his deep knowledge of their own businesses.

At meals he is brilliant. He likes to entertain his guests with history and philosophy, which he can make clear and fascinating to even the most untrained mind. And yet he can talk about mountain scenery like a poet, about actors and orchestra conductors, the design of a carpet, the ingredients of a salad dressing.

He is a vegetarian, eschewing the cruelty of slaughter. His plans for retirement are to return to painting, to leave a few good scenes to the museums of the State as a legacy. It is ironic, is it not, that his soul is essentially Bohemian, artistic, and dreamy. He says that he would have been happy leading a simple life in a garret, seeing his fellow artists in the cafés, brooding endlessly on the mysteries of light and shadow. And yet this mind was the one destiny chose to see the truth of history in clearest perspective, and he did not flinch from Duty when She came with clarion and banner at the moment when Germany took her place foremost among the nations. Germany above all.

His shyness has endeared him to many. Once, when he was a rising politician, he came to the notice of a lady in society who invited him to an evening at her mansion. He came in formal wear, perhaps as a surprise to some of his detractors. He kept his hands folded modestly in his lap, having to refuse the liquors and nicotine periodically offered him by liveried butlers moving among the revellers. Aside from some meaningless chitchat with various socialites, he said nothing all evening until the party was breaking up, when he took a stand near the door and gave a beautiful oration against Jewishness, communism, atheism, lies in the press, and flagrant immorality in entertainment and the arts. The tone of frivolity which had prevailed throughout the festivities was, you can be sure, suddenly sobered. Thoughtful expressions took command of faces which moments before had been heedless and silly. It was a magnificent performance.

There are many accounts of the skeptical going to the Leader's study groups for a lark and of being converted and coming away new men.

He is never at a loss. When he mounted the podium to eulogize Hindenburg at that great man's funeral, he opened his folder to discover that some careless clerk had put in it not his well-chosen words but what seemed to be a financial report from the Gauleiter of Weimar. He spoke *ex tempore* and none of the thousands before him were the wiser.

He can hold his salute for hours when he reviews the army.

He is in perfect health and never sees a doctor except to talk about the health of his people. He and the doctor usually have a good laugh. The German people are so healthy, who needs a doctor?

He is a man of exemplary tolerance. When a deputy once asked if French art was to be brought in line with National Socialist ideals, the reply was:

— Far be it from me to dictate the taste of so witty and accomplished a people!

He thinks the Paris Opéra the most beautiful building in the world. He likes the advanced design of transoceanic steamships and of airplanes. On his table at the Chancellory he likes to have a vase of chrysanthemums resplendent in golden light through the window.

Our minds resonate with his opinions. Spain under Franco will save the

Catholic west as it did in the time of Phillip II. You can detect the stalwartness of the Russian peasant by his bread. Psychoanalysis is Jewish filth impudently trying to pass for science. The Italians are romantic and flamboyant. The German spirit has best been expressed by Wagner. Responsibility and alertness characterize the German, treachery and hypocrisy the Jew, dullness and vapidity the Russian intelligentsia, sloth and mindlessness the American, hauteur and shallowness the English, ignorance and venality the Pole.

Dr. Goebbels hangs on his every word. Goering loves him like a brother. His faithful staff rejoices in his presence.

It is not true that his square moustache is copied from Chaplin, or that the Party rallies derive from the chants and cheers of American football games. The Leader's hobbies are weekends in the mountains, phonograph records, automobiling, home movies, and designing neoclassical buildings. While he listens with every attention to his ministers at conferences, his hand draws triumphal arches on his notepad. He has an ear for the mighty line of Goethe. He is fond of dogs.

Spengler remarks that it is a German trait to be aware of an historical moment while it is happening. Just so. Were words ever so true? There is an electric excitement to the air this October, a sweetness everywhere all about. We are, as always, a scholarly sober people with our dumplings and beer and good fat black blood puddings, our string ensembles, which even in the humblest villages can do memorable evenings of Brahms and Beethoven, our incomparable schools and universities, our youth so strong, healthy, and beautiful. And all is purpose, purpose, a purpose perhaps greater than any ever undertaken since the world began.

And somewhere in this resplendent autumn, along roads glowing with the bronze and red foliage through which they wind, there is the Leader, driven by his proud chauffeur corporal. He loves Germany and knows that Germany loves him. He stops to chat with children, farmers, doting grandmothers, blushing maidens whom he enjoins to bear stout sons for the Fatherland.

Perhaps he has stopped to look in on Frau Elsbeth Förster-Nietzsche, whose passion for all things Teutonic is almost as fervent as his. They sit under the autumn trees in the fine air, with a plate of macaroons and a bottle of Selterswasser. The distinguished sister touches a handkerchief to an eye, remembering Fritz. The Leader sits with his legs comfortably crossed, a pose he permits himself only in the company of his equals and friends. Ordinarily he is shy around women (an astute writer has said that the transcendent idea of Germany is his wife), but with Nietzsche's sister he is at ease.

They feel that his spirit is with them and quote to each other the mighty aphorisms that Frau Förster-Nietzsche compiled in *Der Wille zur Macht*. They know the work off by heart. It is said by privileged witnesses that their voices make a kind of music. Noble minds, noble words, noble hearts! But this idyll for a poet, this conversation piece of historical subject for a painter, does not remain wholly on the level of the sublime. As with all civilized people, they exchange pleasantries, and the Leader's charming laughter is like those jolly phrases from German folk dances and rustic songs that Beethoven in his joy could not suppress from even his most serious compositions.

Might we not, in imparting the essence of the Leader's character to children and students, do well to preserve for them the magic of this autumn afternoon, the high seriousness of the talk under trees so lyrically beautiful, and the very human playfulness of the Leader as he is beguiled by Nietzsche's sister into having another macaroon?

The Bicycle Rider

• I

They could see through the grime of the barnloft windows, Anders and Kim, how far the field of sunflowers they'd walked across stretched down to where the sawgrass begins back of the beach, sunflowers higher than their heads, bitter green and dusty to smell. They could see yellow finches working the panniers, butterflies dipping and fluttering, the glitter and lilac blue of the sea where they'd been horsing around on the sand. They'd filed along the narrow path like Mohawks, Kim brown lean and naked except for the skimpy neat pouch, cinched by string around his hips and down the cleft of his butt, in which his sprouting peter and spongy scrotum made a snippy jut, Anders behind him, a head taller and with a livider tan, his bathing slip a pellucid Danish blue. Jellyfish bit me once, Kim said, his hair like maize silk flopping in a spin as he smiled over his shoulder, and did it ever sting but I didn't cry, brave me, and once I cut my toe on a shell, and got sunburned once real pitiful. Glowed in the dark. They were pals in a Greek goatherd-and-shepherd poem, *idyllisk*. Boldly sneaky, Anders, but with Kim you didn't sneak very far. His blue eyes saw all.

• 2

Macadam road through pines, early morning, a red fox slinking through grass bent with dew, rabbit into bramble. Happiness is a sensual tonality of being, Hugo Tvemunding, assistant classics master at NFS Grundtvig, wrote in his journal after his run. *Le bonheur* was the better word. *Lyksalighed* had northern sharpnesses of light and dark. Luck has nothing to do with happiness, which comes from rhythms, order, clarity. A card from Papa in the mail, and *Der Eisbrecher*. Greek torso, Apollo, third century. *I do hope, dear Hugo, that you're getting this hurt of the unfortunate young man you call the Bicycle Rider behind you. Hurts that cry out to Heaven do not go unheard. The hollyhocks are more beautiful than ever. Come see them, why don't you?*

• 3

Pastor Tvemunding, who was reading H. G. Wells's *The Passionate Friends* in his garden time about with a detective Penguin by Michael Gilbert, after leafing through the *Church Times*, said to his cat Bobine Pellicule, Well, old girl, the letter from Hugo (yes, he's coming to scritch you under the chin) with its question about an aorist in the gospel of Markus made you yawn, though you found the bit about latching onto a young lady of great interest, *jo?* We remember others, do we not? Do we not, indeed.

• 4

I didn't think, Kim said, you'd even notice that I exist, much less make friends. The barn had a grand smell of oats cows chickenfeed old wood and time. They could hear only their steps up the steep ladder to the loft, the nattering of finches in the sunflowers, the white noise of wind and sea. Chinks of blue, Kim's eyes, after he'd said that the yellow light paced along the smooth wide floor in rectangles was beautiful and that the silence was sweet and the barn snug and private. *O jo!* Anders said, cozy secret bright, stepping from window to window. Our place, all our own. Kim turned on a heel, stomped, and took off his cache-sexe, hanging it around his neck. His penis cantered out over a round and compact scrotum, its longish foreskin pursed at the tip. He scrunched his eyes, feeling naughty and in love. Anders, mouth dry, swallowing hard, shoved down his bathing slip, snapped it inside out, and hung it on a peg. Earlybird sharp, eyes rounding, Kim whistled to admire Anders's lifting penis nudging its glans free. *Ih du store!* Skin yours back, Anders said. It's a thumper for twelve. You think? Kim asked.

• 5

This golden flower of Peru, or sunflower, being of many sorts, both higher and lower, with one stalk, without branches, or with many branches, with a black or with a white seed, yet not differing in form of flowers or leaves one from another, but in size only, rises up at the first like a pompion with two leaves, and after two, or four, more leaves are come forth, it rises up into a tall stalk, bearing leaves at several distances on all sides, one above another to the very top, being sometimes seven, eight, or ten foot high with leaves which standing out from the stalk are very large, broad below and pointed at the end, round hard rough, of a sad green, and bending downwards: at the top of the stalk stands one great large and broad flower bowing down its head to the sun, and breaking forth from a great head made of scaly green leaves like a great single marigold having a border of many long yellow leaves, set about a great round yellow thrum in the middle, which are very like short heads of flowers, under every one of which is a seed larger than any seed of the thistles, yet somewhat like, and lesser and rounder than any gourd seed, set in so close and curious a manner that when the seed is taken out, the head with its hollow cells seems very like a honeycomb.

• 6

Rutger, he said, and Rutger he was. Anders invented for his bunched brown curls an adoring mommy, pederast of a barber, and Narcissus complex. We're stuck with each other, Johannes Calvin having laid it on us in his pep talk that getting along with your roommate is character itself. You don't look pukey. Rutger here, and you're? Anders. He wore American jeans, perfect fit, an English plaid cotton shirt, rotten sneakers, germless white wool socks, a French undershirt with skinny straps, and a smidgin of briefs, Hom style micro, with the little triple-flame trademark on the left below the spandex waistband. Out of these he flopped an outsized dick. Lucky you, said Anders. It serves, said Rutger, and stays in tone by coming without let or cease, spurt spout splat. Scrounging in a canvas bag of silver scissors, combs, shampoo, nail clippers, dental floss, toothbrush, orange sticks, he located a green tube of Panalog from which he squeezed gunk that he smeared on his glans. Vaginitis, he explained. From his girl Meg, the second time the sweet slut had given it to him. You've never caught it? An infection that itches like fire and parches the foreskin. He was going to get laid around four, and give it back to Meg, and she back to him. Crazy.

• 7

Nu vel, Anders said, we'd got into our *sammenslynget* when, with sandpipers nittering and pecking and the edge of the sea was sliding the plies of its border back and forth, and that's all the universe was doing in our part of it, except that the sky was being bright summer blue over our heads, and I sweetened my gaze at you and wriggled my toes, you said, you little rascal, Keep looking at me like that and my peter will stand bolt upright and whimper, and I kept looking at you like that, and here's your peter, *herre Jemini!* rose-petal pink, standing bolt upright. So why are you blushing? Robin eggs in gelatin, Kim's balls to Anders's feel. For answer Kim curled his fingers around Anders's rigid haft, squeezing gently, tentatively. It's beautiful, he said. So's yours, Anders said. Do you come yet? I think so, Kim said. I'm not nearly as brave as I want you to think I am. Why do you like me? Because, Anders said, there's a poem by Rimbaud that begins *Aussitôt que l'idée du Déluge se fut rassise, un lièvre s'arrêta dans les sainfoins et les clochettes mouvantes, et dit sa prière à l'arc-en-ciel à travers la toile de l'araignée.* And the dove came back with an olive branch in its foot.

• 8

Here, said Mariana, I've brought you a rose. And I've brought you a weed, Franklin said. Thought it was a flower, but Sissy says it's a weed. Girls are like that, Hugo said, hard to please and never satisfied. *Hejsa!* I'll put them together in the one vase here, to show that I like them both.

• 9

Franklin standing under Hugo's metre-square photograph of Emile-Antoine Bourdelle's *Héraklès archer* (1910) in a thin silver frame was like all the children in the world in museums, their innocence and alert attention virginal before a Mondriaan, a broken Hera, a case of paleolithic axes, a Cubist harmony. A convincing Greek, Hugo said, the cunning of Odysseus, or of a mountain lion, in that muzzle. I think he looks like a possum, Franklin said. What's he shooting? Monsters, said Hugo. All terrible things.

• 10

A glass jar of acorns. A nautilus shell. Shale slab with a fossil gingko leaf. A Greek coin from Metaponton in Sicily. A snail shell. Greek text of Marcus, dictionary, coffee cup, running shorts drying on a hanger hooked to the sky-light latch. Boy Scout Handbook, with markers. Mariana, said Franklin, says she likes this place better than any she's ever been in, and I do too. Sure glad we met you on the beach.

• 11

The greatest of these beautiful thistles has at the first many large and long leaves lying on the ground, very much cut in and divided in many places, even to the middle rib, set with small sharp (but not very strong) thorns or prickles at every corner of the edges, green on the upper side, and whitish underneath: from the middle of these leaves rises up a round stiff stalk, three foot and a half high, set without order with suchlike leaves, bearing at the top of every branch a round hard great head consisting of a number of sharp bearded husks, compact or set close together, of a bluish green color, out of every one of which husks start small whitish blue flowers, with white threads in the middle of them, and rising above them, so that the heads when they are in full flower make a fine show, much delighting those who look at them: after the flowers are past, a seed grows in every one, or the most part of the bearded husks, which still hold their roundness until, being ripe, it opens of itself, and the husks easily fall away one from another, having in them a long white kernel: the root is great and long, blackish on the outside, and dies every year after it has borne seed.

• 12

Kim, home, strayed into his father's study. Before Henricus Hondio's *Nova Totius Terrarum Orbis Geographica ac Hydrographica Tabula*, he smiled at the lion and ox reclined by a pumpkin in the border. Gerardus Mercator Flander. Grapes peaches cucumbers. Like Papa to have so narrow neat and black a frame. Then he stared at the engraving of Holberg to the left of the map and reset the nudge of his penis in his pants. The view through the French windows was a Bonnard. He read all the dull mail on the desk while fitching his crotch with meditative fingerings. At the harpsichord he played a gavotte by Bach, to keep from thinking of Anders just then. Midnote a repeat he froze, swivelled around, and turned a cartwheel. The view through the French windows was Bonnard because of the greens and mauves, the rusty pink of the brick wall. Anders, talking or strolling, liked to roll the ball of his thumb against his dick through his pants, and laugh like a dog about it, no sound, only a happy look and slitty eyes. Kim slid his pants down and off. Whether anybody was home he didn't know. His briefs caught on his shoe and had to be hopped free. He yawned grandly, and stretched. He finished the gavotte at the harpsichord, did another cartwheel, and sauntered upstairs, britchesless. On the bed he allowed himself to think about Anders, happily, wondering if he were wicked, silly, or simply lucky.

• 1 3

How, Mariana said, did you talk a horse out of it? And with accessories to match. I thought only sailors were so gifted. I haven't blushed since I was ten, Hugo said. Are you always so uninhibited, and so generous? Born so, Mariana beamed. Judging character at a glance is my best talent. They were sitting on the free beach, friends of half an hour, Mariana combing her black hair dry, keeping a lookout for Franklin in the shallows. He'd picked up spadger friends and they were idiotically scooping water into each other's faces, squealing, stomping, kicking. Mariana, naked, was on her knees undressing Franklin when Hugo strolled up on the momentum of an impulse he dared not let flag. Hi! he said, Hugo, scoutmaster, schoolteacher, adept at small fry and making friends with beautiful strangers. What do you teach, Mariana asked, weight lifting? She hauled Franklin's jersey over his head, unpantsed and debriefed him, and combed his hair with her fingers. Little brother Franklin, she said. Our day at the beach. Mariana Landarbejder. Work in a kindergarten, with brats. So I get to sunbathe with one. Maybe he'll drown. Hi, brat, Hugo said. Isn't it exciting to have so sweet and good-looking a big sister? Hugo undressed, making a neat stack of his clothes beside Mariana's. You're gorgeous, she said as they trotted into the waves. You're beautiful, he replied. Life can be very simple, Hugo said after their swim. I have a room over the old stables at the school where I teach, wonderfully private, which you're going to like. And I won't ever know if I do or not if I don't come and see, will I?

• 14

Papa? Kim in stubby blue pants all but occulted by a jersey with the collar flicked up cockily in back, fists at thighs, head down. Yes, dear Kim? You're as brown as an Etruscan and as fetching as Ganymedes. Who's that? Charming chap your age in Greek legend filched by Zeus to do God knows what with. Speaking of which, scamp, an hysterical mother, dash it, called to say that you've been exciting the school with jabber about sex. Something she said you said about the rights of children to it in great heaps and doses as a revolution against stuffy middleclass oppression. O my yes, and the red flag down the village road followed by troops of naked youngsters. All of this, and more. My ear was ringing, rather, before she finished. All I ask, Kim my boy, is that you take the persuasions and fiercely guarded decencies of others into consideration. Eh, what? Don't look so damnably glum. I'm only talking reason. And you're not listening. Papa, Kim said, looking up bravely, I'm in love with my friend Anders. We want to sleep together. We've got to. Every night, I mean. In his bed in the dorm, or in my bed. Anders Hammel. He's fifteen. There are other boys here who love each other. They're just like anybody else. Anders is not a sissy or anything. Mama won't even notice.

• 15

Rhinopithecus, a permanent inhabitant of the cold high forests of Moupin, has a very thick fur, like the Macacus. Aeluropus, the most remarkable mammal discovered by Père David and kin to the singular panda (*Aelurus fulgens*) of Nepal, is as large as a bear, the body wholly white, with the feet, ears, and tip of the tail black. It inhabits the highest forests, and is therefore a true Palaearctic animal, as most likely is the Aelurus. Nyctereutes, a curious racoon-like dog, ranges from Canton to North China, the Amoor and Japan. Hydropotes and Lophotragus are small hornless deer confined to

North China. A few additional forms occur in Japan: Urotrichus, a peculiar mole, which is also found in Northwest America; Enhydra, the sea otter of California; and the dormouse (*Myoxus*). Pallas's sandgrouse (*Syrrhaptes paradoxus*), whose native country seems to be the high plains of Northern Asia, but which often abounds near Pekin, astonished European ornithologists in 1863 by appearing in considerable numbers in Central and Western Europe, in every part of Great Britain, and even in Ireland.

• 16

I'm a little drunk with you, Hugo said to Mariana. We began with busting the mattress, which is fun, and now I hear your voice when you aren't here, and smell you in my nostrils, your girl smell and your vanilla panties and that cucumber taste of your breath, milk and cucumber, and see your China-blue eyes when I'm working. Sounds awful, Mariana said. By drunk, Hugo said, I mean I lose my balance a little when, coming from class, I tell myself that I'll see you soon, and kiss and fuck you, and hug you a nice long time afterwards, and then we'll talk, and I'll learn that you've never heard of Ibykos or Li Po or Braque. Greek poet, way back, quinces in one of his poems, and a black wind from. From. Thrace, he said. Thrace, she said. Chinese poet, green rivers, plum blossoms. Braque is a painter. Blobbed mandolins, skinny little clay pipes, anemones in a bowl. Just like Picasso but different. Read Greek, look at Braque, and then go teach Scouts how to tie knots, sheepshank clove hitch stoppers trumpet shoestring and square. Life is very simple, Hugo said, when you know what you're doing. Yes, said Mariana, but I'll bet you don't.

• 17

At Elseus Sophus Bugge they swam naked, boys and girls together, showered together, and learned where babies come from. Good enough, Anders said. And, Kim went on, they learned that *masturbere* is good in moderation, and it was Kim who asked how many times a day is moderate, and why in moderation anyway? Girls had giggled and Kim's friend Karl put his hands over his face and peeked through his fingers. And here, freckles, foxred hair, beaver teeth, and snatchy glances, was *unge hr* Karl in person, brought by Kim to be shown Anders's dick. He comes a handful, Kim said, and it's white and thick. Scrounge it out, Anders, so Karl can see how crazy big it is. Kim's, Anders said, obliging, is going to be a whopper if he keeps it in condition with steady exercise and long workouts. *Aldrig i livet!* said Kim. Karl asked to feel. Sure, Anders said. Kim's friend's my friend, and friends can snug anyway they want, *jo?* Karl swallowed a frog, and said, he'd like to see Anders shoot off. No problem, Anders said. Back of the boathouse, under the willows, where Kim says he used to whack off before we imprinted on each other. Gee whillikers, said Karl. It jumps when he comes, Kim said, and bounces. At Grundtvig they walk around in the dorm in their underpants, some in nothing, and everybody whacks off whenever they want to.

• 18

Who's Grey Eyes here in his birthday suit? Mariana asked of a canvas. That, said Hugo, is the Bicycle Rider. He never came again for me to finish the picture. He was a student here, bone lazy, a day student who lived out on Nordkalksten where, as you know, there are dens of louts mainly American and German, and where the Gospel has not been preached. Pretty nasty place, Mariana said. Creepy. I've seen him about I think. Tall, blond, very pretty face, clothes from the Salvation Army? He was in my Greek Myth class, Hugo said, and by the third day it began to get through to me that he was quite simply the handsomest boy I'd ever seen in my life. But with arrogantly messy hippy hair, and, as you say, oil rags for clothes. A young prince in peasant disguise, I said to myself. And then he had very little to do with anybody, except some students who envied his revolutionary costume and easy cynicism. He was quick to point out to his admirers the particular stupidities of all the faculty, whom he pitied for their stodginess. He was alert in class, though, and could fake the most sincere interest in myths and Greek culture.

• 19

Reindeer across golden moss in a cloud of their own breath, Sibelius. The forest, Kim said lying face down on the bed, talking into the pillow. Snow down the steep sides of fjords. Wolves with silver eyes. A dust of frost in the air that gets up your nose and stings, and tickles the corners of your mouth. He reached under his hips to undo his jeans, buckle, brad, and zipper. Fucking the bed, he worried and wiggled his jeans down to his knees. Bach, he said, dances. Mozart dances. But Sibelius flies. He tried getting his jeans off with a squirm of toe work, hobbling his ankles. Keeping the cadence of his humping steady, he thumbed down his underpants and fidgeted them, wriggle by twitch, as far as the wadded jeans. My wizzle, he croodled, is up so loving touchy stiff that it's got a crick in it. He freed a foot and pushed jeans and briefs off the end of the bed. Imp, Anders said. One deplorable imp. See how long you can keep it up. I hear Rutger down the hall. O wow, Kim said. Rutger. Does he josh you about me? Wait and see, Anders said. Sibelius, Rutger said, and *for guds skyld*, Ven Anders, take Nipper here up on whatever he's pushing.

• 20

The white Mountain Daffodill with Ears rises up with three or four broad leaves, somewhat long, of a whitish green color, among which rises up a stalk a foot and a half high, whereon stands one large flower, and sometimes two, consisting of six white leaves apiece, not very broad, and without any show of yellowness in them, three whereof have usually each of them on the back part, at the bottom upon the one side of them, and not on both, a little small white piece of a leaf like an ear, the other three having none at all: the cup is almost as large, or not much less than the small Nompareille, small at the bottom, and very large, open at the brim, of a fir-yellow color, and sometimes the brims or edges of the cup will have a deeper yellow, as if it were discolored by saffron: the flower is very sweet, the root is great and white, covered with a pale coat or skin, not very black, and is not very apt to increase, seldom giving offsets: neither have I ever gathered seeds, because it passes without bearing any with me.

• 21

Anders husking down his briefs, fighting out of his jersey, stripping loose his shoelaces, said that the black stripe on the neck and feet of archaic horses and asses is called in Greek the *mykla*. From the plains of Poland, Kim said, grasslands from this horizon to the other, the last herds of wild horses in Europe, rounded up like a hundred years ago, *jo?* Lovely big horses, iron grey, nickering and whinnying, up to their knees in Russian pink and Ukrainian blue meadow flowers, frolicking foals and dignified mares. *Hej!* So last night, reading in my sockfeet across from Papa in his fog of burnt applejuice pipesmoke and telling me bits from the paper, what assholes politicians are, my dick began to burrow in my jeans like a perky little mouse. So I nudged it along, by way of petting it, until it was hard as a rib, and throbbing. *Den er mægtig!* We sluddered three jumping slurps out of it over the afternoon, with that crazy bird saying *Well I never! I think so!* in the tree above us, and here he was randy again. And Papa looked funny over the top of his glasses and then up to heaven, and then paid me a wink. O boy. *Lille djævel*, Anders said. You're going to have little nubbly horns growing. One here and one here.

• 22

Six or so, I suppose it was, Hugo said, when an agemate and I, Ole Vinsson, all freckles and towhead, made a scientific study of sexual differentiation, with his sister, who was ten and had a mind both forthright and level. We simply took off our togs and satisfied our curiosity. It was his sister Julie's opinion that whereas God gave babies, people had to love each other to show that they wanted them, and that parents fucked all night long, all day long too, right after they're married, with ineffable pleasure, until God was convinced, and supplied the baby. We found out about her *kildrer*, and she gave us a demonstration of tickling it. She had friends who could tickle themselves into hysterics, passing out with the pleasure of it. Real boys, she gave us to understand, had stiff peters all the time, like the satyrs of old. Surely, Mariana said, you were older, eight or nine? By then, said Hugo, Ole and I had learned from a rangy teenager the fly of whose jeans always seemed to be cordially distended that jacking off makes one's peter grow. Doesn't it? Mariana asked. Don't tell Franklin if it doesn't.

• 23

Squeamish, me? Rutger hooted, towelling down. Meg'll not blink a lash, and like all women is nosey about you and your gamy sweetmeat nipper. Give her a hot crotch maybe even. Anders, well balanced in the articulately inflected fit of his jeans and smug about the sideway wrench of his fly that gapped the top teeth of his zipper and canted out its tab, was in a whickering good humor. Hard balls, he said. Cock growing a bone inside. But, said Rutger, you milked that rowdy last night, and grunted a lot doing it. Twice, said Anders, and got pulled off twice in the dingle, by untuckering boypower, a tongue in overdrive, and an everloving will. Does he pant, Rutger said, when he sees your dick rearing up, like Meg? Says her heart lurches. What if I'm turned on by your pukey kid and his pink little sprig of a weewee? Every man his specialty, as you say. Whereupon Kim stomped in, hair tousled, and got hugged by Anders and, wickedly, by Rutger. I think I'm scared, Kim said, judging by one cold shiver or another I keep getting. Makes it spicier, said Rutger. Meg's setting out about now. We meet her at the bend and head for the boathouse. Then we all fuck and whatever it is you do until we pass out with coming. And then go at it again, gasping and weak, squish squish. Crazy, said Kim.

• 24

Through the hornbeam and beech forests of Transylvania and the Djerdap Gorge, the Danube over seething rapids, white shoals, falls, foaming sluices, comes to the whirlpool of Lepenski Vir. Here, on a ledge above it, lived an epipaleolithic people whose vestiges Dragoslav Srejović found in 1960. Their community sat on a horseshoe shelf above the great spiral of water, with the steep cliffs of the Koršo Mountains at its back. Among apron-shaped houses laid out like steps stood monumental Erewhonian statues whose faces groan with the agony of birth, or with awe before some wonder or terror. The endemic plants were lilac smokewood manna ash slow buckthorn Dalmatian toadflax cypress spurge oxeye camomile. Bone bracelets needles awls. The dead were buried as if giving birth, the skull of a stag over the shoulders. A frieze of geese on a pot, deer in a thicket. Ovens altars hearths were decorated with wave patterns. Elk and salmon, and the navel of the river below. Owl in the hornbeam was father's sister's daughter, red-combed quail mother's brother's son, celt hook lilac, lilac circle spinning water. Night rain, noon rain. Salmon river, bear wood.

• 25

He was a pleasant interest, Hugo said. I like people. He was moreover poor, taking courses at NFS Grundtvig as a day student on tuition from a government grant, parents divorced, making him eligible for a stipend for the disadvantaged. He had the one pair of ratty jeans, a few secondhand shirts, and perhaps not enough to eat. So the first time I invited him over, ostensibly for a drawing, I laid in sausages, beer, cold ham, a potato salad, a melon. He was charming. It was his second time over that I learned he slept in a large box in a hallway. This he rented from a hack freelance artist, gay, unfortunate personality. By the third visit I'd decided to move him in with me. There's room. So I said, Bring your traps. He said that the idea of sharing quarters with me was like a dream. He would have all these books to read. Engines in the switching yard would not wake him before dawn. No hideous fights among toughs in the street outside one's window. No cockroaches. He was to move in on the Wednesday. I waited in a nice excitement. I like new things, new turns. I knew it would be difficult having him here. What did I know about him, really? Pretty much nothing, except that he needed taking in. I waited and waited. He never came.

• 26

Six Ryvitas, Mariana gasped. And came like a brass band passing the royal box on Liberation Day. Franklin at his lookout was chinning on a limb, up and down like a puppet on elastic strings. *Det hele?* he called. *Forbi.* The river's not the ocean, Hugo had said. Drop in, holding your nose, bob up, and I've got you. Hang on around my neck and I'll swim you out to the sandbar. Your own island. Here he danced out some intricate fantasy, crouching, springing, kicking water, falling down shot, rebounding to repulse ten insectoid invaders from another galaxy with laser spurts. *Zonk, zink, zonk.* Ferried back twice now to stand guard while they fucked, jeans rolled to pillow Mariana's bottom. At Skordbærbjerg, experimental school for brats and trendies, Mariana said, run you know by worldsavers and psychologists, there was this little nipper of a girl, all of ten, going up and down the hall holding her twat, naked as a newt, and in her free hand two Ryvitas and a krone, which she was offering to whoever for a fuck. Fun was, the look on the face of some government functionary inspecting the school that day, who had already seen two teenagers doing it in the library and half the kids naked in the pool, and had been propositioned by a boy with a twinge of pubic hair if you looked close.

• 27

Bunce, Hugo said. Five kilometers, ten lengths of the pool, and I find a girl looking hopeful on my doorstep and her little brother, The Rabbit Who Invented Electricity, looking bored. He wants to go to the beach, Mariana said. Does his big sister? Hugo proposed the river instead. Is it textile? Oh no, there're boys there from school naked as they came into the world, and as innocent, and as loud. Lay out croissants and jam while I shower, Hugo said, and explain why I'm happily lecherous so early on a Saturday. Crazy, I guess, Mariana said. It is standing sort of straight out, isn't it? And slipping its big pink head out of its hood. A cold shower? Mariana suggested. Pure thoughts? Shower with you, Franklin said, untying his shoes. Two cold showers, Mariana said, and shall I make coffee, and why do I have a monkey for a brother? Is that him there, under the suds? Grit your teeth, Hugo said, cold rinse, needle spray. They both howled, falsetto and baritone. Nobody, Franklin said, has dried me in ages. Lean over and I'll dry you next. Not only did your dick not wilt in the shower, Mariana said, but now the little shaver has his up, too. Lovely, said Hugo. Let's bounce the bedsprings, eat, and go to the river. I'll eat all the breakfast, Franklin said, and hide my eyes and think pure thoughts if my pizzle will let me.

• 28

I'll understand it, Mariana said. You too, but not him. Yes, said Hugo, but you have given me the bow of Hercules. Didn't need to give you his balls, Mariana said.

• 29

So Muggins came over here the first time to be sketched, Mariana said, and radiated charm from wall to wall? He was two hours late, Hugo said. I didn't recognize the sign at the time. He explained, when I asked him to, that he met somebody on the way he wanted to talk to. I'm listening, Mariana said. I'd made supper, which he picked at. He posed well enough, and I got two good drawings. We talked about all sorts of things over beer afterwards. He recited a poem, rather awful, but with expression.

• 30

In moments of sweet clarity, Hugo said, I doubt if we can communicate at all. You mean one thing, I hear another, benignly in banter, violently in an argument. But, said Mariana, we've never had an argument. Of course not, Hugo said, and don't intend to. I mean that human beings probably can't make each other understand what they mean. We have to get our meaning from art, from writing. That's awful, Mariana said.

• 31

Rutger barefoot on his shoulders, Anders stood, all the way to tiptoe. A fingerhold on the sill and Rutger monkeyed up the wall. A heave, and he was in Meg's room. He blew a kiss to Anders in the dark. Hours later he shinnied through his own window at NFS Grundtvig, feet wet with dew, in briefs only, hair tangled. Anders, Kim asleep in his arms cheek to cheek, woke and whispered *hi!* Rutger wrapped himself in a blanket and sat beside the bed. Came three juicy everlastingly sweet ballcramping times, on a pallet, as the bed sounds like a tin wheelbarrow loaded with kettles over cobbles, Meg's roommate obligingly away. Then, just as they were in the heaves and wild thumping of the third fuck, there was some species of Gorgon stalking the hall and opening doors. He'd just had time to pull on briefs and drop from the window. Passed a rabbit, he said, but I turned an ankle somewhere along the way and hopped the last fifteen or so meters. My feet are ruined forever. Isn't it time for Nipper there to be decanted from your bed and sent home? You look wonderful, Anders said, with your hair all a charming mess.

• 32

Meadows, Anders said. If I could write a poem it would be about a meadow. A symphony, Kim said. Only music could get the feel of a meadow, I think. Monet, Rutger said, painted lots of meadows, and Pissarro. Lots of painters. Russians, Norwegians, they're good at meadows. So what do I say? Kim asked, who had to write an essay on meadows. Sunday afternoon, Meg visiting her parents, they were walking in the long meadow that flowed speckled with wildflowers and butterflies down from the knoll back of the wood to the river. Us and those cows yonder, Anders said, we have the world to ourselves. I love quiet. Be inventive: say the *long* quiet of a meadow, the green minty grassy smell. They sat. Kim took off his shoes and socks. Kim's brown as a nut all over, Anders said, the brownest he's ever been. Anders pulled off Kim's jersey, standing over him and hauling it up inside out over rolling bony shoulders. Bare feet in clover and daisies, he said, I'll put that in. Wild strawberries, chickweed, darnel, cowflop. He stood by caprice and doffed his britches. Baby in his nappies, Rutger said. A sight, said Anders. Baby out of his nappies, Kim said, tossing his briefs in the air. See, Anders said, nutbrown all over. You're going to have a cock, Rutger said. Why do we wear clothes, Kim asked, when it feels so good to have air all over you? To keep people from going crazy looking at you, Anders said.

• 3 3

I like my sandbar, Franklin said, like my river. Also Hugo's house all one room and a big window in the roof. Sand on your dick and balls, Mariana said, brushing. And, said Franklin, you and Hugo have come three times and I've only come once. *Hejsa!* that feels yummy. This isn't icky? Hope not, Hugo answered for her. But, said Franklin, his eyes squeezing closed, acute pleasure making his fingers spread and his mouth a muzzle, when she lollies your dick you're kissing her between the legs, and then you fuck. *Oh jo,* Hugo said, sweet and slow. Hunch in, and you'll get a flutter of tongue-tip on the backdrag. Warm and wet, Franklin said, and good. Me next, Hugo said. Mariana shooed him away, smoothing hands up Franklin's thighs to his collarbones. Faunulus on the mossbank, Pastorella on her knees. The blithering phone. *Hallo, jo.* Not really: an afternoon with friends. Love to, but can't. Later, then, or another time. Bore's delight, the telephone. Going to come, Franklin said. Coming! he sang. Figmilk, said Mariana, a nice skeet and a fribble. What a blush! Hugo hefted him out of the chair and crushed him in a hug. Bet you, he said, you can't come again, two handrunning, and then we'll all be even, and start over.

• 34

His top lip jibbed out and tucked at the corners by baby fat, lively eyes speculative and fluttery by spells, Kim laughed at Anders's bashfulness. He was at the bus stop, as they'd agreed, in, as Anders said, the world's shortest pants, book satchel foolishly balanced on his head, coquettish looks out of the sides of his eyes. Anders slid his bike sideways right to his toes, radiant, breathless. Eyes met, but they said nothing. Kim on the seat holding him by the waist, Anders biked off down the macadam road that went through the woods. Only when they'd reached the beech copse with high ferns and moss clearing did Anders say, And how was school? Just school, Kim said. We're going to have sensitivity classes, so we'll be aware of our bodies, and our space, this teacher, she's a woman, said, I think her name is Miss Pumpkin or Squash or Beanvine. Girls have boney hips, do you know? I'm going to like geography and in Danish we have to learn some kind of dumb poem about Iceland. Are we going to take our pants off? I guess I was feeling my peter through my pants when we were standing around, because teacher frowned and shook her head. Did you jack off last night? But yes, Anders said, and yesterday afternoon, and a long time at both. It's out here some- where that Rutger fucks Meg into fits. Have you fucked girls? Kim asked.

• 3 5

Well, she said, you're crazy. Some crazies are a misery to themselves, and some a nuisance to the world, but you've figured out a shipshape Calvinist glitch-free craziness in absolute kilter, so that your eyes fly open at six, you hit the floor like an Olympic champion, hard-on and all, jump into a dinky pair of shorts, jog three kilometers, swim ten lengths of the gym pool, nip back here for wheatgerm carrot smush while reading Greek, communing with your charming freckle-nosed *kammerat* Jesus, shower with unreason- able thoroughness while singing hymns, dress in a French shirt and Amer- ican tie, English jacket and experienced jeans that show how horsily you're hung, teach your classes, Latin, gym, and Greek, meet me, pretend you're interested in what I've done while eating me with your eyes, bring me here for wiggling sixtynine on the bed, tongue like an eel, melt my brain, fuck me simpleminded, race off and instruct your Boy Scouts in virtue, knots, and nutritive weeds, sprint back here, fuck me into a fit, teach me English while fixing supper, show me slides of Monet and Montaigne, fuck me again, walk me home, make eyes at Franklin, come back and read two books at once, say your prayers, jack off for an hour, and sleep like a lambkin. It isn't bright, you know.

• 36

Gustav, said Mariana on her back in clover and daisies, chewing a leaf of mint, big brown eyes, thatch of hair always washed and feathery. Handful of balls and a stout stubby dick. And Jorgen his buddy, blond as a duckling, long all over, long chin, long forehead, long legs, long peter, big feet. Stammered something horrendous. Gustav finished his sentences for him. We had a rabbit hole of a place, cozy inside under brambles. Crawled in on hands and knees. A snuggery of great privacy, though a bit crowded with the three of us. And from the military academy across the way, Hjalmar, who rammed and grunted and was fitted out like the assistant classics master at NFS Grundtvig, or a horse.

• 37

In Argentina, Anders said, they arrest people who have read Einstein, torture them with electric shocks through the dick or cunt, and drop them while they're still alive from a helicopter into a marsh outside Buenos Aires. They're doing this *now*, forty years after Buchenwald. A Russian truck driver has just been arrested for owning a copy of the poet Mandelstam printed in the west, and given seven years hard labor in Siberia. Einstein! He was a Jew, you see, and the church tells the fat-necked military that his physics threatens to undermine belief. The USA has enough atomic bombs to blow the planet into orbiting rubble. And all these bullies want to idiotize us into thinking of all affection except that decreed by the state as immoral. Pigs, Kim said. Anders said: Don't insult pigs.

• 38

Tom Agernkop, strand of hair across an eye, signaled Anders with a look and confirming nod. So Anders followed him to the far edge of the soccer field. You saw us, Tom said, picking a blade of grass and chewing it, Lemuel and me, hugging in the shower. Anders shrugged. Your business entirely, he said. Who've you told? Nobody. What's to tell? Rutger my roommate, maybe. A mouthbreather, Tom. Meaty upper lip, Greek nose, honest eyes. Look, it's fine by me, Anders said. Nothing scary about it. You love each other. Tom grunted, squeezed his crotch, flipped his hair out of his eyes, talked. It just happened, he sighed. It's very good, tender, exciting. It's terrific to be so close to him. We're each other, you know? And he's so fucking good-looking and good-natured. We were real dimwits, at first, hot blushes and cold feet. That was dumb. Now, though, we're out to love each other into feeblemindedness, like maybe they'll have to carry us limp to a home, with permanent smiles on our faces. You're giving me ideas, Anders said, and also a hard-on. *Gud!* Can I tell Lemuel? Who is it? Let me ask him before I tell you, OK? But absolutely, Tom said. Lucky, whoever he is.

• 39

The housemaster Holger Sigurjonsson with Pascal in tow looked in by way of bedcheck, Rutger towelling his hair, Anders writing in his journal. Pascal, seven-eighths naked and slender as a greyhound, grubbing at the pod of his briefs, broke off his discourse on trilobites and the planet Mars to inspect the girls on Rutger's wall. How goes it, you two? the housemaster said to give Pascal his fill of the pictures. *Tosset!* Anders said, standing to thumb down his briefs. Rimbaud in French, Mimnermos in Greek, and gameto-phytes in botany. What's this girl doing? Pascal asked. O the infants around this place! Rutger said. She's whiffling her *kildrer* and coming like Beetho-ven's *niende*. What did you think she was doing? Got me, Pascal said, I'm cryptogonadal still. Iceland, Middelhavet, and Bornholm, he said of three maps on Anders's wall, and you, Anders, stark naked. Is that your blue grizzly tent? *Hej!* that's Kim Eglund with you. He's neat. Fellow baby, said Rutger. Who are these kids with their peepees standing out? Swedes, Anders said, riffling Pascal's hayrick hair. With it, the housemaster said. Come on, Pascal. OK, Boss, Pascal said, trying to read a bit of Anders's journal while being herded out by Rutger.

• 40

The disk of the Medusae is as truly an abactinal structure as the calyx of the Crinoids. As in all Discophorae, the substance of the disk is a gelatinous mass, consisting of immense cells, the caudate prolongations of which tra-verse it in different directions, assuming the appearance of flat muscular fibres. But this appearance is deceptive, and the substance of the disk does not, in reality, contain distinct muscles, though it is highly contractile, especially in the thinner part of the margin. Its movements are owing to the structure of the lower floor. The amount of water contained in the tissue of the disk is truly extraordinary. A specimen, weighing thirty-five pounds, exposed to evaporation, left a viscous mass, chiefly composed of common salt, showing the water to be common seawater. The salt having been washed out with fresh water, and the organic substance dried simply in the sun, weighed less than an ounce. For all its pellucid grace and unearthly subtlety of curtained tentacles and hyaline genitalia in radial clusters on a cincture, the Cyanea jellyfish is little more than organized water.

• 4 I

Owl call low and clear after bedcheck and lights out. Rutger said, There's your boyo. Quit looking like a calf that's lost its mama and haul him in through the window. Skinned a knee, Kim whispered after he'd been hugged hard and was shucking his briefs, but the rope works fine. He stripped in moonlight, Anders lifting the sheet for him to skittle into bed. Let's see the knee, Rutger said. I've got iodine. A hard-on already. That's the spirit. Yee-ouch! Like don't pour the whole bottle on, Rutger friend, huh? Keep the bedclothes over you, Rutger said, tucking them in and mussing Kim's hair, so that I don't get ideas or a skeet of sperm in my eye. Love good. Did you, Kim asked, do it with Meg this afternoon? Twice, Rutger said. With our jeans under her butt in the ferns, after the foreplay of the century, talk about fine tuning. I hear snurfling, I hear Kim sighing. We love you too, Rutger, Kim said.

• 4 2

So, said Hugo, Tom. Come in: timing's perfect. I've come at a bad time, Tom said with a robin's hop of blinks and rueful smile. Not a bit of it, Hugo said pulling on denim shorts and combing his hair with his fingers. My Mariana and I were just getting out of the sack when you knocked. Hi! said Mariana shoving her arms into Hugo's shirt, modern times and all that. You've seen scads of stitchless girls before, and maybe one or two in hr. Tvemunding's bed. I couldn't be the first. Tom, uneasy but boldly shy, sheep snarls in the silkfloss hanks of his rascal hair, his scruffy shirt parting at the shoulder seams, tail out in one side, shuffled, forced his big hands into the pockets of his jeans shorts, looked hacked, and sat with a bounce when Hugo pushed him into a chair. Here, said Mariana, *pariser* leftbank intellectual coffee with four sugarcubes in it, did I guess right? *Mange tak*, said Tom. So? Hugo said, you look demented. When, said Tom, can I come back? Right now, Hugo said. Frøken Landarbejder, besides being the soul of discretion, will probably understand you better than I. If that's the way you want it, hr. Tvemunding, Tom said, miffed. Tom! Hugo said, relax, eh? We're all friends. Some of us, Lemuel and I and a few more, want to start a club for friends who love each other, and we need a faculty sponsor with balls and a very broad mind, Tom said. Our part in the Revolution, you know. Revolution, Hugo said, ah yes, the Revolution. Sounds wild, Mariana said. Explain it all.

•43

Anders had sat cockminded through the dullest English class of the century, besotted with Kim's grubby sneakers that made his feet too big, like a puppy's outsized paws, socks, dinky short pants, net briefs with their narrow midseamed cotton panel in front, his toes, legs, the celts of his knees, his springy supple peter growing like a weed. Gym, its perfunctions. Lunch, raisin pudding yet again. A wink from Tom. Kim, brash devil, scrunched the crotch of his snippety jeans shorts as Anders reached the bus stop on his bike. The high ferns, spackle light and green shadow through the beeches, Kim tumbling down his briefs and into Anders's hug, they breathed in the same measure, rubbing noses, grazing lips, touching tonguetips. You're crazy, you know, Kim whispered, but you've got to stay crazy. I know, Anders said. Even before lights out last night, I began jacking off, to keep our afternoon yesterday in my head, some of which I told Rutger, and kept it up, and didn't see any point in quitting. So it rained sperm all night on my side of the room. I got a second wind toward sunrise, a fever in my dick, my balls sore, but your eyes looking sideways, like now, kept me going. Toes, smile, knees.

•44

Quick, Rutger said, standing to slip off his briefs. Our keeper and Chipmunk. Check, said Anders, whippering his dick to a lolling halfminded erection. *Pok pok pok!* Pascal was saying as he spun in, turning on his heels, the explorer craft from outer space, *swoosh*, has come to bed check, where are we? Ah yes, Rutger and Anders. Commander Sigurjonsson! Hi boys, said the housemaster. O wow! said Pascal, new pictures. On Rutger's wall an athletic youngster fucking a deliciously shapely girl whose enthusiasm was unqualified, on Anders's a towheaded skyblue-eyed summerbronzed naked adolescent with a lucky penis and plump scrotum. Pascal, flicking his fingers on his ribs, inspected both. The housemaster sighed. Rutger leaned in a long stretch from his chair, caught Pascal by the hips, turned him around, and yanked down his piffling underpants. Just looking, he said. I'm slow, Pascal said. You should help it along, Rutger said, forefinger and thumb. In moderation, the housemaster said, looking troubled. Show me, said Pascal. You have the highest IQ in all of NFS Grundtvig, Rutger said, and don't know how to play with your peter? It's retarded, Pascal said.

• 45

What I didn't know, *stor* Hugo, Mariana said, was what a hideaway from the world your place is. Freedom itself, Hugo said, nidge away, sweet girl. She'd turned up bushed, with Franklin, pitched her jeans across the room, flopped into the big reading chair, nudged down her flimsy underpants, and begun to quiddle her *kildrer*, to jolt off the kicker she'd been playing toward all day. Woke up horny, she said, worked it to a buzz, and then off and on, two minutes here and five there, a sweet shiver and a tickly ripple. Franklin, Hugo's scout hat over his ears and eyes, was trying to crack limbs for kindling over his knee like Hugo, who was laying a fire before which they were to eat. Sitting on the floor, Franklin said with approval, all beside each other, sandwiches and milk and pickles. But first, Spejder Franklin, I must hug and kiss Mariana awhile, and get hugged and kissed. Why don't you see how much more firewood you can pick up over beyond the soccer field? Can I wear your hat? Absolutely, Hugo said. Let me tighten the strap and tie your shoe.

• 46

OK, said Franklin, two armloads of firewood. Admirable spadger, Hugo said. Your smart generous pretty sexy sweet sister says we can fall upon our supper, soon as I light the fire and lay things out, or you can have your dink jiggled to your heart's content, so you won't feel left out, *jo?* Franklin, Mariana said, is the only little brother in the world who can fake a blush and say *honest?* with such innocence. What he means, Hugo said pulling on a sweater and hooking his briefs off the floor with a toe, is that he chooses to grub by the fire. Not really, Franklin said. O yes, but really, Mariana said, throwing cushions toward the hearth. Nothing like both, Hugo said. Fire's catching good. Mariana laying out plates and glasses, Hugo fetching eats. Franklin wriggled down his pants, which would not then go over his shoes. Hugo obligingly unlaced them, pried them off socks and all, and made a neat stack of shoes, socks, pants, and underpants beside Franklin. Nice pinkish-brown peter, he said. As soon as Franklin comes, Mariana said, he starts over. Mouth full of pressed veal and orange slices, Franklin grumped contentedly, stripped his foreskin back, and drank deep from his milk. Plop him between us, Mariana said, and we'll take time about. Did you fuck good? Franklin asked politely. Mariana leaned around and kissed him on the nose, which wrinkled.

• 47

This place, Meg said, could use a broom driven by a strong and busy elbow, and a mop, and all the windows open the whole of a breezy day. What it really needs, Rutger said, is two mattresses lifted in the old Danish manner from the supply room. My knees survived the sand last summer, and forest-floor grit, moss, sticks, and boulder rubble, but these pine planks are going to sandpaper them raw. They'd unfolded and laid out a sail, the area of which brought them chummily together, so that Meg, thoroughly fucked and wrung limp by a whalloping sweet orgasm, could reach over and muss Kim's hair and tickle the back of his neck. Modesty, she'd said when they were undressing, sort of has to be dispensed with, *jo?* Kim, pulling his jersey over his head with his back to her while Anders untied his sneakers and slid down his briefs, did a military about-face, with eyes shut and a broad smile. O what a charming pink blush! she said, pulling him into a hug. Timidly he hugged back, and then hugged warmly, with a kiss for her nose. She returned the kiss on his navel, and gave him up to Anders's claiming arms.

• 48

If you put it that way, Hugo said, then yes I was a fool. But it pleased me to be a fool. In the dark you learn by bumping into things. But, Mariana said, he knew what you would bump into. He knew what would hurt you. I taught him, all unknowing, Hugo said, how to hurt me. That turned out to be his style: to listen in silence and a mask of charming innocence, and lay in wait. Because that's all he had: the power to hurt. Don't ask me why. It's a gratuitous meanness that's everywhere nowadays. In people without character, it's a passive vindictiveness. They are too lazy and unmotivated to be evil actively, that's too much trouble for the drifting will. But if opportunity puts anything alive in their path, they kill it, for the idle sport of it. To care about anything is a threat to their slothful passivity, so carelessness becomes the only plan you can see in their liquid will. If you encounter a flower bed, trample it. It's the casualness of their hate that's so discouraging. No, Mariana said, it's the difference. What you say is true, but what makes you hurt inside is how different this trashy kid is from everything that's familiar to you. You give people things, and this kid smilingly accepted what you gave him and smashed it with his foot before your eyes.

• 49

What we have, Hugo said, is an unfinished room with good proportions and pleasant light once we wash these windows as clean and bright as Perrier water. No other NFS Grundtvig clubroom will be half so spiffy modern. We can sandpaper the floor to a plain Shakerish natural finish. Composition boards for walls. Let's paint everything white overhead except the rafters, which want to be Mondriaan Red, *jo?* on the uprights and Sailor Suit Blue on the beams. What else do we want? No chairs, Tom said, but maybe a table? A bookshelf, posters, slogans painted right onto the composition board. Danish Spartan it all needs to be. OK, Hugo said, let's see it with work, then. Lemuel'll be here in a bit, Tom said, and Kim and Anders later. Composition board to be delivered tomorrow. So let's sweep and scrub and haul junk out and cancel cobwebs. We want the outside stairs painted, too, and the door. Danish Blue. Light bulbs, a journal for minutes, paint, sandpaper, Windex, rags, detergent, a pail, hard brushes, hammers, nails, a roll of white gummed stripping. Ho, Anders! Ho, Kim! With brooms. And Rutger! I like cleaning things, Rutger said. Don't get ideas. I'm here as an enemy of dust and a lover of straight lines and clean surfaces.

• 50

God knew exactly where he lived. In among all those warehouses and dockside pubs. The school had his mother's address only, and she had no phone. My feelings were hurt, I suppose: snubbed. But that was an afterthought. I was anxious, befuddled. What I discovered two days later was that he had simply forgotten. He'd run into an old friend that Wednesday afternoon that he was to move in, when I was to make the effort to do something about him, give him a home, feed him, make a close friend of him. When I finally saw him, he grinned nonchalantly. He was, he said, thinking about my offer to take him in. Why had he not called or signalled for two days? I said, Look. People don't act like this. O I'm a shit, he said. Besides, your kind of structured middleclass life is not mine. It's against my Buddhist principles to live on a schedule. Your Buddhist principles! These, it turned out, he'd acquired from McTaggart's Transcendental Meditation Group, which he'd twice attended. McTaggart is one of the English masters, and has his group. He talks a lot of bilge which, because of its gaseous vagueness, appeals to the feebleminded, ladies from town, slobs, prigs, and nonstarters of all sorts. A free spirit, said my Bicycle Rider, blows about like a leaf in the wind.

• 51

Tidsskriftet Hermes. Ih! Letters from Oskar and Papa. *Nature, Arkaeologi,* Haydn's *Mass in Time of War,* hollyhocks, a sermon on responsiveness, a twinge of rheumatism, and some jolly good damson preserves. Oskar into the antinuke protests, a salt-free diet, and a Swedish girl's knickers. A cycling-capped blond *purk,* alert blue eyes, *pik* dangling through his open jeans, smiled a cocky grin from the cover of *Hermes. Meget vel!* Hugo said to himself on a *15årig* inside, *splitternøgen* and healthy as a horse, heel of right thumb along shaft of distended penis, ball of thumb on glans, fingers curled underneath and partly around, face faunish, nose pert, eyebrows arched, feathery eyelashes lowered in gaze at penis, at least 18 cm, foreskin rolled back of glans in a fat wet crumpled ruck, the thick stalk ridged with callopy wales branched over by a relief of veins, glans in snubby profile glossy with a slick of bulbourethral drool. On his bike, with a buddy. And, three pages along, wilted and content on a sleeping bag on a forest floor, he gazes amiably, with a nacreous splash beside his left nipple, a milky spatter across his midriff, and a puddle of cloudy egg white on his abdomen, with runnels into his scant crimp of pubic hair and into his navel.

• 52

If the Angraecum in its native forests secretes more nectar than did the vigorous plants sent me by Mr. Bateman, so that the nectary ever becomes filled, small moths might obtain their share, but they would not benefit the plant. The pollinia would not be withdrawn until some huge moth, and with a wonderfully long proboscis, tried to drain the last drop. If such great moths were to become extinct in Madagascar, assuredly the Angraecum would become extinct. On the other hand, as the nectar, at least in the lower part of the nectary, is stored safe from the depredation of other insects, the extinction of the Angraecum would probably be a serious loss to these moths. We can thus understand how the astonishing length of the nectary had been acquired by successive modifications. As certain moths of Madagascar became larger through natural selection in relation to their general conditions of life, either in the larval or mature state, or as the proboscis alone was lengthened to obtain honey from the Angraecum, those orchids which compelled the moths to insert their proboscides up to the very base would be best fertilized.

• 53

Kim, the blue bill of his red cycling cap turned up, and Tom, his amiably mussed hair brilliant under the steep pitch of Hugo's skylight, sat on the bed. Anders, hugging his knees, and Hugo, holding his elbows, head down, listening, agreeing with nods and doubting with his shoulders, sat on the floor. Lemuel, thumbs in the belt loops of his short pants, stood and talked. As I see it, he said, we'll be just another school club like Botany, Greenpeace, or Hiking. Hr. Tvemunding is, *Gud være lovet*, our faculty sponsor. Hugo, said Hugo. In class, in the gym, in the quad, hr. Tvemunding, but in the fellowship of the club, Hugo, please. And before we proceed, let's do what I have my scouts do, all of us hug each other. Us too! said Mariana, arriving with Franklin. Mariana and Hugo with tongues in each other's mouths,

Mariana and Anders with an awkward squeeze, Mariana and Kim friendli-
ly, Mariana and Lemuel warmly, Mariana and Tom sweetly, Mariana and
Franklin with a kiss bravely consented to and wiped off. Hugo and Anders
robustly, with a soldierly kiss on the cheek, Hugo and Kim timidly but repeated boldly, Hugo and Lemuel tightly, Hugo and Tom sexily, Hugo and
Franklin (when caught) recklessly, with squeals.

• 54

Anders and Kim chastely, nubbling noses, until a *nej hør nu* from Tom,
whereupon they kissed with closed eyes and roaming hands, Anders and
Lemuel, spiritedly, Anders and Tom, brashly, Anders and Franklin auda-
ciously. Kim and Lemuel confidently, Kim and Tom with madcap indiscre-
tion, Kim and Franklin impishly, prodding each other's crotches. Lemuel
and Tom with easy affection, Lemuel and Franklin outrageously, with hoots
and promiscuous kisses and tickles and goosings and a roll across the floor.
Tom joined in, capturing Franklin from Lemuel, who captured him back,
with the loss of a sneaker. His jersey ruckled to his chin and his britches half
off, Franklin, howling that he was being kissed to death, wrenched a gym
shoe off Lemuel and tugged Tom's shirt over his face. *Oh ho!* Lemuel hooted,
pinning Franklin in a hug while Tom deprived him of his britches, and on
second thought, unzipped and hauled off Lemuel's, too. Us against him! said
Lemuel to Franklin, and they threw Tom and debreeched and deshirted him.

• 55

Pentstemon Glaber, Pursh. Very glabrous, leaves usually glaucous, sessile,
entire, the cauline lanceolate or ovate-lanceolate. Flowers large, in a thyrsoid
panicle, sepals broadly ovate, submembranous upon the margin, obtuse or
more or less pointed. Corolla bright purple, widely dilated above, the limb
shortly two-lobed, with the lobes rounded and spreading equally. Anthers
loosely hairy or glabrous, the divaricate cells dehiscent from the base nearly
to the summit, but not expanded. Sterile filament short and hirsute towards
the apex, or glabrous. Specimens accord nearly with Var. *Occidentalis* Gray
(*P. speciosus*, Dougl.), having the anthers and sterile filament glabrous and
the leaves often narrow, the numerous violet-purple flowers an inch or more
in length. Washington Territory (Douglas) and Nevada (Beckwith, Stretch).
Frequent in the valleys and foothills from the Trinity to the Havallah Moun-

tains, Nevada, 5 to 7000 feet altitude, May–June. Var. *Utahensis*. Stems straight and slender, cauline leaves long, oblanceolate, tapering to the clasping base, sepals ovate-acuminate, not at all membranous, anthers and sterile filament hirsute.

• 56

Stitch of bronze midges over daisies, bees working wild hyacinths, butterflies yellow and white nuzzling clover at the meadow's edge, Kim and Anders glistening wet rolled their shoulders and stretched like limbering gymnasts to dry in the hot light and sweet air from the river. Lovely, hr. Sigurjonsson called from the spit, joining them with Pascal astride his shoulders, a skinny *basunengel* whose wet eyelashes gave a look of wild freshness to his teasing gaze. You're like the picture in your room, Anders, he said, you and Kim on that beach. That was last summer, Anders said, when we became friends. And, the housemaster said, you've been fast friends ever since. Jacobsen says, I believe in *Niels Lyhne*, that the tenderest and noblest affection is that of boys for each other. It is both warm and shy, not quite daring to show itself with a hug, a glance, or in words. It's all tacit, reluctant, anxious. Beautifully, it is a fusion of admiration, selfless generosity, loyalty, and a great quiet happiness. Got it in one, said Anders, sliding his arm across Kim's shoulders, Kim an arm across his. *Opkastig*, said Pascal. Do that again. Whereupon the housemaster lifted Pascal down and lay in the sun on the spit. *Sludder*, said Pascal, and bosh. Pascal, said the housemaster, don't be a snob.

• 57

Guess what, Mariana said. Mom was out for the night with her friend the toothbrush moustache and I was reading a bit before dropping off. *Unge hr.* Franklin was mucking around with the stamps and album you gave him, like a lamb in clover, and then here he was in nothing but his nightshirt and best cherub's grin, climbing into bed with me. So what the heck. A hug is a hug, and the essential differences in anatomy that he explored by hand come under the heading of education. The little devil, Hugo said. And then what did you do? Explored back, she said, and jacked him off thoroughly, but not so thoroughly that he didn't repeat the pleasure while I hugged him, with the odd kiss on the cheek or a nice puff in his hair. And then we fell asleep. He's comfortable to have in bed, and smells good. He acted grown-up this morning, and kept offering me things at breakfast, as polite as if feeling his sister's breasts had civilized him more than all the shouting at him I've done over the years. Perhaps we've discovered something? He also said, though it's not the first time, that he thinks you're great, and wonders if you like him as much as he likes you. Of course I like Franklin, Hugo said, he's our Cupid.

• 58

Meadow flowers, Kim said, hard yellow buttons, white stars, blue bells tight against stalks, pinks and purples. Nations of gnats, mists of midges sawing through the air. Are you enlisting nature to excite your dick? Rutger asked. He lay drowsy and shirtless beside Anders. *Mna*, Kim said, my hand strays when I'm bare-assed. It is, now that you mention it, feeling good. Anders beckoned him with a crooked finger. *Ak ja*, Rutger said, our *englebarn* is going to sprinkle the meadow with his own personal dribble, three whole drops. Kim crawled between them, flopped on his back, nestling his head on Anders's shoulder, sprawling his spread legs over theirs. He gawked at Rutger eye to eye, and at Anders, who licked the tip of his nose. Sunday afternoon in the middle of the meadow, he said to the sky. Rutger slid his hand down Kim's abdomen, nipped his penis between two fingers, and played it in a wobble. *Hejsa!* Anders said. Cool it, Rutger said, I'm only being friendly, though it's interesting that my prick seems to be making an unseemly display of its manly size. Woof! said Kim, you're good. I'm blushing, Anders said. Rutger sat up, for better purchase. When it's feeling really lovely, he said, Anders can take over. What a happy grin. Rutger, Kim said, is our best friend, isn't he, Anders?

• 59

The Bicycle Rider was as unresponsive as God. The young are in their own minds immortal, and assume Olympian indifference to their own deaths. They die drunk on dormitory floors, in automobile wrecks, hundreds a day, on futile battlefields, needles under their tongues, in their arms, in epileptic seizures for want of a fix, but this violent and pitiful mortality does not disturb their liquid minds any more than the screams of the dying at Waterloo caught the attention of the geese in the sky above them.

• 60

Neither *la poussière olympique* nor the waters of Galilee had touched him. He partook of nothing Hugo could eventually recognize. He had found a new way to be inhuman. His face, a harmony of Scandinavian lines and Slavic planes, gave no hint of his addiction to lysergic acid, from age twelve, or of his cold hatred of his family, of his delight to hurt.

• 61

He was thinking, he said out of the blue the last time he was here to pose, of laying off the acid for awhile. He'd had forty-one hits in the previous five weeks, thirty in the past three. Indulgence, yes, he said, but not indulgence carried to the extreme. Lysergic acid diethylamide, a wheat smut that corrodes synapses in the brain while binding with its tissues, causing the delusions of dementia praecox. Using it is deliberately simulating a senile deterioration of the mind. The pushers on Nordkalksten cut it with strychnine, and with speed. He was willing to endure stomach cramps that bit his guts for days to have these waking bad dreams that he called mind-expanding. *Shit* was what I said. What else, said Mariana, was there to say?

• 62

He would come home through the vicious traffic of Nordkalksten on his bicycle, carry it up back stairs in an alley. A hovel, when I saw it. Trash everywhere. Britchesless, for the acid was his sex, he would melt a tab of the acid under his tongue, whacking off, beginning to see the world through a tacky snow of purple and silver flakes, lines bending, volumes swelling and diminishing, all colors mixing with yellow. There was a feeling of grand euphoria, of well-being, of success, of being immensely clever and wise and at peace. Drunk, said Mariana. Drunk is drunk.

• 63

Pallets, said Tom. *Ak jo*, pallets. Aren't they neat? Yes, said Hugo, but where did they come from? Well, said Tom, you know Asgar Thomsen, third year thickshock cornblond gymnast type? And you know Elsa, works in the kitchen, fifteen or sixteen, with the stickup breasts and sliding eyes? Well, those two fuck their brains out in the laundry room, never miss a day. Elsa knows where all sorts of things are, like a stash of gear from when NFS Grundtvig ran a nursery, and these pallets are from that, nippers' naptime pallets. They fold up Japanese tidy. Elsa, eh? *Jo*, Tom said. Asgar says she's great. She loves giving wee boys their first pussy, and is a good teacher, and likes five or six at a go, but her soft spot is for big Asgar. God knows what goes on at this school, Hugo said. Let's hang the Otto Meyer here, with the Hajo Ortil, what say? North and South. Swiss Boy Scouts in a summer meadow all daisies, lots of skinny brown legs, three bare butts, two thumb-sized dicks. Norwegian Scouts in Sicily, one of Ortil's expeditions of *teutonsk* youngsters big and little. Greek boy with hoop and rooster in the middle. Posters coming from Düsseldorf, Tom said. Anders's doing, that. Radical Left rights-of-kids' stuff. Wide-eyed German idealism.

• 64

Tjajkovskij, said Mariana, pulling off a tall sock. I can listen to him. Teach me English. And French. What's the good of getting laid by a teacher, never mind one with shoulders like the Stock Exchange and a peter like a pony, if I don't learn something. *Kiss*, he said, and demonstrated. *Kiss on the tit.* Plural, *tits.* You're slurpy wet, Hugo observed. Because, she said, I was playing with myself waiting for you. Passed out twice. It depraves Franklin, who wiggles out his grub and whisks it to a blur, great egg-beating technique.

• 65

He was, the Bicycle Rider, trying to feel. That's what makes your hair stand up on your head. Trying to feel. What began with some jaded old fools, Aldous Huxley, a giggling British neurotic, moral idiots like Burroughs and the poet Ginsberg, and the shit-for-brains Timothy Leary, what began for them as a desperate attempt to feel something, anything at all I suppose, became an initiation of the young into feeling. Young who had not yet felt love or wonder or surprise or the use of their minds learning math or Greek or history took their little trips on acid. Death, of course, is something that happens to other people. To talk crazy and act crazy is chic.

• 66

Nose like a buck hare, said Hugo. Square toes. Eyes slyly sweet and sweetly sly. Hugo, liking the world, was an accurate draughtsman. Franklin sat on a chair, elf naked. You see? said Mariana, there's nothing to it. If you get the giggles, you get the giggles. Hugo can wait. You can kick your heels when he's drawing your face, and roll your head like a moron when he's drawing your feet. I'll tell you what to keep still. What you going to do with the picture? Franklin asked. Look at it when I need to throw up, Hugo said. *O Gud!* Mariana said, the giggles. It's going to be a good painting.

• 67

This. He told me. One day in class, listening to me lecture on Greek myth, his mind was following but it was also anticipating jacking off while stoned later that afternoon. LSD, you know, binds with the brain and is a permanent chemical activity of it. It volunteers hits weeks after you've had any of it. It rarely volunteers the euphoria of good trips, preferring nightmares. So the satyr's leer in his gray eyes changed suddenly to cold fear. He was, while still hearing me on the bow of Herakles, facing a classmate who has hit him, cutting his lip, unsocketing a tooth that bleeds salty and hot. He must swallow the blood and try to focus his courage and twining eyesight, neither cooperating, and then a surge of desire drenches his balls and tingles in his lifting glans. He holds back a wave of nausea. The loose tooth bleeds freely. The taste of blood sickens him. He must jack off. He can't trust himself to stand and leave the classroom. His bowels seem to have a knife through them, cutting. He'll walk into the wall. The bully who hit him stands nose to nose whispering insults. Fairy, cocksucker, flit. His throat is full of blood. Sissy, morphadite, jerker off. If he could get to the hall, he could puke there, green phlegm that the acid makes. He could jack off in the hall, fuck who'd see him. With acid time is elastic. Class would last another four hours. Or two seconds. And all I saw was a handsome Scandinavian face with a charming vagueness in the eyes.

• 68

Something's in there hurting, Mariana said, pushing into Hugo's chest with both hands. Something that needs to be healed. You're doing it, Hugo said, holding her close. Let me tell you this, and we won't mention the Bicycle Rider again, *jo*? I made the one last attempt to make friends with him, to show him a world he could see and feel and live in once he'd got his head out of his ass. I found out where he lived, even went there twice, and I wrote him a letter offering to take him along on a visit I'd planned to Paris, my favorite city. I'd pay for everything. All he had to do was come along. No answer to my letter. I ran into him (he had no phone, naturally) one day a week later and asked him, with some annoyance, if he'd got my letter. O yeah, man, he said, airily. That's great. Paris, France! You're a good man, you know. Denmark was such a backward hole of a country. He'd always longed to see Paris. He would go with me, and split when we got there, and he'd meet me for coming back. I didn't believe my ears.

• 69

In our time Apollo is sound asleep.

• 70

You have been my best teacher, he said. I'd love to take your inhibitions away from you. My inhibitions! You're not free, man. We had a wild talk. He had made me mad, confused me. So I'm a shithead, he said. What's that got to do with anything? A good exchange of name-calling cleared the air. Generosity, I can see looking back, was simply not in him. He'd put the worst construction on all my friendliness, and now that I knew he was on dope I felt a kind of mission to save him. I insisted that he come to Paris. We would look, walk, see all the beautiful city. I would get him out of himself, his head out of his ass. He would see. I showed him slides, books. He agreed to go. I gave him a big hug, and he froze, saying that he wasn't used to affection. So what happened? Mariana asked. Nothing, said Hugo. We met a few times, always by accident, as he would never turn up when he would say he would, made plans. I was to meet him here and we'd go together to the train station. He never came.

• 71

I went over to his place after going to the train station to see if the white-trash slut might have decided to meet me there. These neosixties young imagine that you know what they're thinking, and can't be bothered to tell you. I found him eating cold mashed potatoes and rice in a dirty bowl. He was naked except for a hospital gown, the kind they put on you for surgery. Hi, he said. He was eating with his fingers. Where the hell were you! I shouted at him. Man, I feel good, he said. Don't shout at me. I had this cold clot in my brain but I'm melting it out, you know? All I know, I said, is that you were to meet me at nine. Why didn't you, where were you, what the fuck do you mean by all this? I'm unstructured, man, he said. I'll go to your crazy Paris with you, but not today. I've got to decide for myself when I want to go. I'll let you know. Do that, I said sweetly, and left.

• 72

Magnus, one of my Scouts, said Hugo of a boy whose hair, blond as a lamb, curled in swashes and scrolls over his forehead. Pectorals in robust definition, he was otherwise as lean as a whippet. Hi, Mariana said, you're pretty. Don't dress on my account. Micro undies are more than I usually see on Grundtviggers. Look, Magnus, Hugo said, even though you're blushing already and going miserable again, I'm going to lay your problem out for my Mariana, sweetest of women. It'll do you wonders. All ears, said Mariana, if there's a stray orange juice, coffee, and roll about. Greengage jam and fresh butter too, Hugo said. We've just been glupping it. Magnus here, stout chap, turned up last night in the grips of a crisis. Beat around the bush, he did, for the longest, and then scared me witless by pitching right out of his chair in a roll, onto the floor, where he bawled like a baby. Wow, said Mariana. Puberty, Hugo said strolling about and stretching, good old puberty. And, as more than likely, our balls charged with manly juices and our unruly cock made our heart tick *allegro* and hanker to hug somebody and be hugged. Oof! and sweet Magnus had tied himself into knots because it's his own gender he likes. I'm horrified, Mariana said, and think I'll faint. You see? Hugo said. She's going to barf.

• 73

So Magnus and I talked for hours. I called his folks and said it was too late for him to walk home and that I'd put him up for the night. Heard that one, Mariana said. Please, Hugo said. And *ho!* here's Tom. Mariana Sweety Pie, Tom said, giving her a kiss. What's all this about, Hugo? I got your note. Magnus Pennystykke, said Hugo, Tom Agernkop: be friends. Magnus is a Spartan, and a little confused. You and Lemuel might, good fellows that you are, show him how friendship works. Don't you have a buddy? Tom asked. We have a club. It's in pairs. What's fun, Mariana said, is two big rascals like Tom and Lemuel hugging like bears and kissing like puppies. Imprinting, it's called. Sex, said Tom. Love, said Hugo. All of the above, Mariana said.

• 74

For the clubhouse, two large photographs, gift of Hugo: Brancusi's *L'Embrace*, which Tom named "The Kissing Boxes," and Picasso's *Tête d'une Femme* in the churchyard of St. Germain des Prés, his tribute to Guillaume Apollinaire. He had bought them to flank his *Héraklès archer* but thought they belonged on the walls of the clubhouse, offering a prize for the best paper on why they were appropriate.

• 75

Tom's beautiful, said Lemuel. See how his neck fits into the muscles of the collarbone and shoulder triangle, and those dogleg lines from hip to dick, they're neat. What if Tvemunding likes boys? He's always talking about ancient Greek sentimental loyalties, as he calls them, and then there're his Scouts, but next he's off on Jesus and Sankt Paul, and he has that dark-haired girl he's most certainly fucking. So? said Anders, why can't he like both, love both? I like girls, but right now don't love one. I love hr. Kim here. If you don't love somebody, you end up loving yourself, or hating yourself because you're afraid to love, or because you're scared to. People are hysterical about sex, anyway.

• 76

This, O Bicycle Rider. That the acid, which binds itself with the fatty tissues of the brain, may have displaced you altogether. When you showed no interest in taking our trip to France, I was up the good part of a night trying to answer why a young man would prefer the roach kingdoms of Nordkalksten to the bright avenues and parks of Paris. What I arrived at is that you can no longer feel anything without this damnable LSD, and that what you've been reinforcing with it (cowardly evading God knows what)—sex, I suppose, as that's all you've told me about—has been wholly replaced by chemically induced neural hallucinations, so that what you think is sex (or reflection, or thought) is only LSD, or marijuana, or the cocaine you say you want to come by if only you can. That is, you limply decline so rich an experience as France because you know that you cannot feel it, cannot observe it: you can only take this diabolic acid along, and feel that. You have built a wall of concrete shit between yourself and reality. This you call sensory enhancement: it is sensory deprivation. You call it mind-expanding: it shrivels the mind to a pinpoint. The mind, Sartre said, is not what it is, it is what it is not. With LSD you ask the mind to be itself only, not the world it can observe. You have your head up your ass, deep in shit. It hurts me to say these things, but I can't live with myself if I don't. When I see you I don't any longer know if it's you or the acid I'm talking to. You are coquettish about visits and conversations and meals and walks, the things we began with when I thought your problems were only loneliness and a proud poverty. Your time, I now know, is the acid's, not yours to share. What frightens and disgusts me is the sudden turn to a limp and feminine unresponsiveness. I'm concerned that you've lost all self-respect: a sane person would be ashamed of such lazy, characterless passivity. I scarcely have any hope anymore that I might be your friend, with exchanges of ideas, walks, trips abroad, letters, meals: all those things that sociable and happy people have always valued. A psychiatrist with whom I've talked about you says that you won't seek help, or respond to it, until much later, when this addiction becomes intolerable. By then you will have no feeling of experience to remember when you're detoxicated, and very likely no mind, either. I can forgive all your shitty, erratic behavior now that I know it was the acid and not you. It was you and not the acid who drew *The Apple that Ate the Serpant* on my terrace, and came and talked afterwards. The theme of your drawing was, of course, temptation, and you were trying to tell me (why me is something I can't answer) that temptation had got you into a bind where all is perverse (turned around the wrong way, is what that word means). Snakes offer apples in the myth, apples cannot eat serpents. There's a wonderful passage in the Bible, in *Acts*, where a devil speaks from inside a possessed person. For devil read Perverse Personality, if you want. It says, Paul I know, and Jesus I know, but who are you? Let's, if only as a figure of speech, say that the displacement of person that happens when you drop acid is a devil. It wasn't even in your *voice* that you said to me the morning we were to leave for Paris and you didn't show up, *I don't know you.* I'm glad the acid doesn't know me. But you know me. I have a strong suspicion that the acid won't allow you to know me, for it is jealous of its power to steal your capacity to feel. It doesn't want me to give you a friendly hug, for that implies comradeship and tenderness and understanding, and these human things it hates as furiously as the Devil hates all love and friendship and kindness and responsiveness. Your beloved acid is a master of seduction, and will have no rivals however innocent. It does not want you to feel French country roads. It wants you zonked out of your mind in that graveyard you say you like to go to when you've taken a hit. It wants you to be lonely and friendless. It is all the friend you need. Why sit in a Parisian café, with all the fun of talking and learning and seeing, when you can be puking frogspawn all of a night in a filthy toilet on Nordkalksten, and endure three days of unrelenting cramps from strychnine poisoning? Why respond to anybody's love when you have your acid for a friend? It understands you, doesn't it? You don't have to try to communicate with it all those tedious things friends like to talk about. You don't have to keep appointments, or have manners, or be generous, and most of all you don't have to respond. The acid is quite happy with your limp, feminine, lazy, self-indulgent unresponsiveness. It knows how to possess.

• 77

Oh but we had some lovely walks, Hugo said, when I thought we were beginning to be friends. I liked his company, his handsome presence, and the

more I learned about him, the more a kind of paternal, or big brother's solicitude grew in me. He'd been expelled twice from schools, for fighting,
though I now wonder if fighting is the truth. More like pushing, Mariana
said. What you won't admit, big Hugo, is that this kid was white trash. I
don't mean that he started that way. I mean that he chose to be white trash.
It's important to them, the student riffraff crowd, to be hateful. That's why
they take dope. But, Hugo said, he was wonderfully sweet and sensitive.
After our walks, he'd say Thanks for the comradeship. I'd say Tomorrow
afternoon, around three? And of course he wouldn't turn up.

• 78

Emanzipation, to Anders in the mail. He thought it would never come. Düsseldorf postmark. Federal Republic stamp with house on it, blue envelope.
Printed Matter: Educational. Two boys on cover, 10 and 12 mayhap, arms
over each other's shoulders, 10 beaver-toothed, naked, full head of hair, foreskin down and puckered to a point, 12 in red billcap and undershirt, pubic
hair beginning, foreskin back, smiling. *Emma für Kinder*. Inside, two teen-
ers at summer camp holding each other's dicks, tents and naked boys in
background, forest trees, green sunlight. Pinewoods, canoes, swallow-tailed
flags on short poles. Norwegian boy with great suntan and lank blond hair
having his big erect dick admired by a fetching nipper all taffy curls deer's
eyes long legs and thumb's up of a peter sticking out of blue briefs' fly. What,
said Kim when it was shown him, does all this German say? Friendship and
affection, bonded loyalties. Fun. I'm glad it says fun, Kim said. Full-page
close-up penis, meaty head as big and smooth as an egg, olive gray pink.
Something about a brother. Dieter and Axel, 13 and 15, looking as innocent
as dogs in their jeans and University of Northwestern T-shirts. Good stuff,
Kim said. Who's this old man in the silver-rimmed specs and Nazi crewcut?
And this supergerman fourth-former with a grub for a peter.

• 79

Which what's that? Mariana crossed her eyes and gave at the knees. Soccer
shorts for little Franklin. Can he get in them? Chalk blue. Are you, she said,
trying to curl up with the adorable monster, his dimples and dink, and kiss
him all over? He'd like that, Hugo said, unbuttoning her blouse.

• 80

Friends, unlike your acid, do not possess. They possess things together, books, films, experiences, moments, fellowship, joys, triumphs, fun, talk, places. You cannot share the experience of the acid. Higher consciousness, you call it. Jesus! What could it add to a work of art, to a place of importance? I have, O Bicycle Rider, wept at the monument to the Deportation, a Kafka-like and grim and pitiful place in Paris where some sixty thousand Jews were loaded onto boats to be taken to their death at Drancy. There's a small light in a long crypt for every Jew deported. I've sunk to my knees there and wept. What would you feel in this place? Would the stupid acid feel sympathy, terror, pity? Charity, as best I can guess, is not one of the acid's specialties. It can fake neural events like sex and euphoria, but of solicitude for others it knows nothing. It doesn't tolerate others. It would not have allowed you to weep for a hideous injustice. This is, shall we say, obscene. Higher consciousness, from McTaggart's phony Buddhism and transcendental meditation to hallucinatory drugs, is trendy Drug Culture Doublespeak for no consciousness at all. My psychiatrist friend says that an addiction as long-standing and ingrown as yours cannot be reached by persuasion or treatment. He says that when this preference for deadness rather than responsive liveliness has become a boring terror and aching intolerable misery to you, only then will you try to free yourself of its jealous possession. I know, and admit, that I'm talking from the outside, but it may be useful to you, if the acid will let you hear these words, to know what you look like. The acid has already made you schizoid: all science agrees that this is what it does. This word means split. I have no doubt that the acid allows you to feel that being schizoid is romantic, free-spirited, and privileged beyond dull clunks like me. I have only my Mariana, that delightful girl, and my classical scholarship, and my Boy Scouts, and my sober round of reading, gymnastics, my thesis for the Theological Faculty at the university, my painting, teaching, learning. I can share what I feel. Not always well, but the possibility is there. I believe what the Boy Scout Manual says: Forget Yourself. The important thing to me is to know, so that I can respond, how others experience being, love, lust, food, a film, a summer afternoon. I try to paint because I want to show others what I think is beautiful. I know by now that the acid won't let you respond. I liked you, saw you as interesting and in need of a friend. I took the trouble to reach out. I still don't want to believe that these fucking hellish vegetable acids delta-9-tetrahydrocannibinol and lysergic acid diethylamide have made you so stupid that you can't get your head out of your ass long enough to talk to another human being, and perhaps even to respond.

• 81

Hi Anders! Hi Kim! We're doing wildflowers, have seen a bunny, and a perfectly round ring of mushrooms. It was Pascal, with Housemaster Sigurjonsson. What are you doing? Mucking about, Anders said. Hello, hr. Sigurjonsson. Fine afternoon, said the housemaster. Pascal and I were making our way to the sandspit for a dip: join us. Looks out of tails of eyes, and *Sure!* Our bikes are over there. We'll come around by the road and meet you, OK? Pascal had found a turtle when they reached the spit and the housemaster was doing breaststrokes and frog kicks in the river. The reason, Pascal said, you shouldn't make a pet of a turtle is that he can't digest his food if he's the wrong temperature. And, as with snakes, you can't tell from their eyes what they're thinking. Why are you undressing Kim, can't he do it himself? Don't splash me, I hate water, and it's cold.

• 82

Germans in their city parks, Anders said undressing on his pallet. There was this bare-chested boy, California tan, jeans with zipper maybe on the fritz, maybe just down, front of his briefs jutting through, like those little balls sacs back in history. Codpieces, said Tom. Had a barefoot friend in short pants of no matter, student cap, like 13, I'd say. Shot Zipper offed his jeans right in front of a line of girls naked as sardines all turning from hot pink to gingerbread brown right before your eyes. Student Cap dropped his little pants, Adam before the Fall beneath. And, being Germans, very serious about it all.

• 83

No absolute petrographical distinction is attached to the terms Berkshire schist and Rensselaer grit. The upper part of the east side of the plateau, its southeastern, western, and northern faces, and its top, consist of grit or graywacke, a dark green, exceedingly tough, and in some places calcareous, generally thick-bedded granular rock, in which the quartz grains are apparent, and, upon closer inspection, the feldspar grains. Numerous veins of quartz, and sometimes of epidote, traverse it. This rock is, however, interbedded with strata of purplish or greenish slate (phyllite), varying in thickness from a few inches to perhaps a hundred feet. A small section, measured south of Bowman Pond, in Sandlake, shows, beginning above, fine grit five feet, slate eight inches, coarse grit fifteen feet, slate one foot six inches, fine grit five feet, slate eight inches. About a mile north-northeast of Black Pond, in Stephentown, surrounded by grit, is a mass of slate six hundred feet in width which belongs either to the grit or the Berkshire schist. There is a considerable area of green phyllite at West Stephentown and of the purple northwest of Black Pond. The thin purple phyllite layers along the west edge of the plateau, in Poestenkill, contain minute branching annelid trails.

• 84

Forest light on bare butts. Kim smelled of mint between the toes.

• 85

Silver look from the hornbeam's Athena strix. Yellow eyes, Pan. Herds of boys, agemates, in Sparta, ate together on the floor of the mess, with their fingers, from the bare boards. They wore as their only clothing winter and summer an old shirt that left their legs bare from crotch to toe, handed down from elder brothers, the nastier snagged daubed patched and too small, the better. They learned together grammar, law, manners, and singing. Each herd had a Boymaster, who taught them to march in time to the flute and lyre. Each boy sooner or later was caught by an older lover, and carried away to the country. The boy's friends came along, too, for the fun of it. This outing lasted through three full moons, and thereafter the two were friends for life. The lover gave the beloved, as was required by Spartan law, a wine cup, shield, sword, soldier's cape, and an ox. With the ox he threw a banquet, and invited all of his herd, together with their lovers, and gave an account, in intimate detail, of how he had been loved for two months. After this, the beloved wore respectable clothes given him by his lover. They went hunting and dancing together, and ran together in races.

• 86

This was our discovery, Rutger said, Anders's and Kim's and Meg's and mine. I know, I know: your club is for superrevolutionary Kids' Rights underage snuggling and jacking off, but just because my pal happens to be a girl is no reason I can see for you to blackball us. Man, look at this red! Kim, a smudge of blue paint across his nose and his hair bound with a piratical bandana, said he voted for Meg and Rutger to be admitted. Meg taught me and Anders how to French kiss. She's done it with a girl, so she's like one of us, kind of, right?

• 87

Morale, said Tom. Openness, brashness, spirit. Boundaries of freedom moving outwards. Put that down in the minutes, Hugo said. What I think, Anders said, is that with all the rockets and megadeath bombs and poverty and violence and fanaticism, Lebanon Ulster Nicaragua Honduras Afghanistan Poland Libya, whole bunches of us need to say there are better revolutions. Talk about simplistic, Lemuel said, O my. When we lose our sense of history, Hugo said, reasoning becomes a lucid madness. That's Piet Mondriaan, the painter. He sat at the feet of the mathematician Brunschvicg, who said, *The more a man imagines himself independent of history, the more, on the contrary, he makes himself its prisoner.* So let's learn some history.

• 88

Blue café awnings winter square Paris trees gray buildings green shutters and Rimbaud in a tightjeaned boy with curls and broad shoulders. Order is freedom, order is grace. The centurion's child (Günther Zuntz's essay, Stanley Spencer's painting). Cock upslant warped bell flare to glans. Deep slick. In the park Mariana leaned an ear for a whisper in birdy sibilances from Franklin, shifty of eye and grin. My word's my word, she said. He won't bat an eye. He's for gosh sakes a scoutmaster and knows all about boys, understands boys. He even likes them. Franklin, dubious, heel to toe, deepened his pockets.

• 89

Headmaster Eglund, Kim's father, a Latinist who had written about Cicero and Seneca, was an authority on classical weights and measures. Or, as Kim's mother the gardener always said, amounts. My dear husband studies Grecian amounts. He had welcomed young Tvemunding after choosing him from among many applicants, and bragged about him to colleagues at other schools. And here was a beautiful essay by Tvemunding on Virgil and St. Paul, their ideals of magnanimity and courage. He called him in. Do you, he said over tea, think there is enough rascal in my Kim? His sister, did Hugo know, was married and with children of her own, his brothers were an engineer in the navy, exec. officer on a submarine, and a graduate student in chemistry. Kim, our Eros, was an afterthought on a second honeymoon in Italy, begotten on a sunny afternoon in a village inn from the windows of which they could see a hill slope with shepherds and goats, an olive grove and a farm that seemed, as it might be, Horace's. Life does beautiful things once in a while, what? O decidedly, Hugo said. But, said Eglund, he's in love, as he calls it, with dear Anders, a gentle boy and a bright one. We know from psychology that this is all properly inevitable, and it has done wonders for Kim. He feels so good about it, and he has been so manly and honest. You work with Scouts and run a well-disciplined and effective classroom. What do you think? It's beautiful, Hugo said. Quite, what I say, said Eglund. I try not to be puritanical. They've started this club, and have put you down as faculty sponsor, and have renovated the old boathouse. Should I look in on it, give it my blessing, do you think? Not without announcing when you're coming, Hugo said, believe me. What would I see? Eglund asked. Come in, dear, he said to his wife pulling off gardening gloves. Classics Master Tvemunding, she said, how delightful.

• 90

Green world. They'd come through deep ferns from the country road, and then up to a ledge of flat rock velvety with moss, hefting their bikes on their shoulders. Lemuel's hair, as blond as Kim's, spiked out in warps from under his racing cap, which he still wore after putting every other stitch neatly rolled in his rucksack, its provender unpacked and lined just as neatly by his bicycle: thermos of cold milk, apples, blue cheese and onion sandwiches, chocolate bars, and a tin of oysters in their liquor. Oysters, Anders said. Oysters, said Tom. To make us hornier, so they say. You swallow them whole, very sexy, with some of the juice. Raw, said Kim. Raw. What an absolutely lovely place. Anders squatted to undo Kim's shoes and pants. You undress him? Lemuel said. Neat. *Hejsa!* the kid has no more pubic hair than an infant. I do too, Kim said, some. He comes, Anders said, and I love him. You're kissing, Kim said to Lemuel and Tom, like a boy and a girl.

• 9 1

Kim was a wolf, weight on four paws like a table, ears cupped and keen. A green frog, hopping. Anders, creeping up from behind, flopped on him, pinning his arms. His nose, a wolf's, could savor the grassy suet odor of a rabbit's spoor, the hairy stink of a dog, the fermented turnip reek of a bear, all the mellow pollen green turpentine bitterbutter acorn smells of the woods, dark smells of punk lichen leafmold. In bed, sleep taking him, he could be a hedgehog, a badger.

• 9 2

Lizard, the Greeks called it, Hugo said, flipping Kim's penis with a nonchalant finger. We didn't think, Anders said, you'd come up when we weren't having a formal meeting. But Tom asked me, Hugo said. I've seen everything anyhow. I wanted, said Tom, to see if you'd come. I don't see anything but some bare boys such as I see thrice weekly with my Scouts, Hugo said. Officially I'm not here. And I must skedaddle in a bit, to meet my Mariana. Kim's the lucky one here, jumping the gun by several years. You met Anders last summer? His folks' summer place is near ours, Kim said. The first time we undressed together to swim, he asked if I knew how to jack off, and I said O yes! And did I? O yes! Lots? O yes! Then, Anders said, he did a stomp dance, snapped his fingers, and whistled, and flopped his hair about. He had seen me throwing my javelin and jogging and reading under a tree and had come over and said he was Kim, eleven, soon to be twelve. I think he thought I was generous to notice him at all. Fifteen is pretty scary, Kim said. So after all the things you do to make friends, we found a sunny old barnloft across a field of sunflowers, where we proposed to do some serious jacking off. I remember that my dick was hard as a bone when I took off my swimslip and had a thrum of benevolence in it. Veins and knots all over it, Kim said. And juice beading out. Bulbourethral secretion, Hugo said, to be coolly pedantic. What an afternoon, Kim said. And all the ones since.

• 93

Rutger's slow eyes' sliding look at Meg makes her hold her breasts with squeezing fingers, red snicks in grass halms fusing their green with mauves and browns. Rutger's quick eyes' bolting look at Meg makes her caress her breasts with fingertips, blue glints in grass halms fusing their green with yellows and blues. Rutger's slitted eyes' satyr's look at Meg makes her knead her breasts with tight fingers, green tones on grass halms fusing their pale straw with tan and cream. Rutger's sly eyes' longing look at Meg makes her pinch her nipples, yellow bosses on grass halms fusing their cedar green with dusk and dew.

• 94

A slope of daffodils down to the river. Old trees. One of those days when Kim was full of himself. Spin and stomp! Spin on your left foot, stomp on your right. He was, he said, into imagination soak. He could be a rabbit, a fox, a mouflon, a cow. Rimbaud's rabbit, Anders said, looking through a spiderweb strung with dew in a meadow. Dürer's handsome Belgian hare, Peter Rabbit in his red jacket and blue slippers, and what's imagination soak? When you see what was always there for the first time, Kim said, you know? The way you see it is to imagine you're something else, like a dog. A dog sees up, and low, and when I'm dogminded I look at the ground, and at the undersides of things, bike seats, chairs, to see how a dog sees it. And, really hard, to do imagination soak and try to be, say, Master Tvemunding, who knows the history of everything, and would see people completely different. He must see me as a squirt with lots of blond hair, and his girlfriend Mariana looks at me and wonders if my diapers are wet. Do you know Mendelssohn's *Reformation* Symphony? When it's raining, but the sun's shining, and you see the sun through chestnut leaves, and you're walking along wet flagstones, doesn't a shiver tickle up your neck? Tell me about Sven Asgarsen again, huh? Anders a freshman at NFS Grundtvig had fallen in love with

Sven Asgarsen a quiet muddleheaded sophomore who loved animals, spoke in riddles, and was out of it. Who are you? he said one day to Anders, who had hitherto studied Sven's good looks from afar and who answered with his name. No no! Names won't do. Science or books? City or farm? Anders said: Books, city, though I've milked a cow and slopped pigs. So Anders learned how to talk with Sven. Pigs, their breeds and who raised them and how and why, flop or stand of ear, curl of tail, rake of trotters. Then goats, bantams, cows. You didn't do anything? Kim asked. I just worshipped, Anders said. And one day he went home. Folks came for him, just like that. I'd never been so lonely in my life.

• 95

Friend of mine from way back is on shore leave, Mariana said on the phone. I really ought to be nice to him. Will you understand? I'll try, Hugo said. The other thing, she said, is that Franklin needs a place to sleep tonight. He shouldn't be by himself. Mommy's off somewhere. Bring him over, Hugo said. Better still, I'll come get him. I won't be replaced? she said. Can't promise, Hugo said. If Franklin looks at me with those big eyes, I may kiss him black and blue. Wiggle his toes, she said, he likes that better.

• 96

Going to fetch Franklin, he remembered at the foot of the stairs the evening he'd come out for a breath of fresh air and found the rider drawing in colored chalk on the concrete terrace. An apple, a snake. He'd lettered around it, *The Apple that Ate the Serpant*. That, said Hugo, is not the way to spell *serpent*. The rider said, I was going to draw it and go away. For you to find. And, said Hugo, what does it mean? Don't you know? the rider asked, all charming smile and handsome eyes.

• 97

Hugo, having graded a set of Greek papers (conditionals, optatives) and a set of Latin (ablatives and datives), written his father (Schillebeeckx, a promise to visit with Mariana while the hollyhocks were at their best, Scouts), washed bowl plate glass and tableware, realizing that it was no effort to be generous toward Mariana, her generosity being enough for them both, set out to meet her and Franklin. No *Apple that Ate the Serpant* on the terrace at the foot of the outside steps, only clean concrete with a cricket in a corner, a beech leaf in the center. The friend from way back was a sailor with a neat wide box of a nose, flat cheeks, good looking, trim. Seems, he said in his handshake, I'm lucky to see Mariana without knowing six languages. Glad to know ya, fella. The same, said Hugo. Franklin and I are going to dare each other to eat a banana split on the way back, the *deluxe extraordinaire* with everything on it, topped with Chantilly and the Danish flag. Then we're going to have a wild evening of dissipation playing checkers. And we intend to have silly dreams.

• 98

Franklin, full of banana split, was going to be a Scout, both a Cub (*Dyb! Dyb! Dyb!*) in a blue uniform with yellow neckerchief, and the mascot to Hugo's troop, going with them on all hikes and campings-out. Moreover, he and Hugo were going to sleep together, like buddies, no pyjamas. In the morning they were going to run four kilometers before breakfast. Hugo was his big friend.

• 99

They were asleep, Franklin's head on Hugo's shoulder, arm across his chest, when a steady tapping at the door woke Hugo. Mariana, would you believe. O wow, she said, naked and all. O, I'm here because sacking out with Hjalmar all night seemed wrong. He has changed, people do. He's as good a lover as always, proved it twice, to be friends. His feelings aren't hurt. Sailors are tough. I belong here. The bed will be sort of crowded, Hugo said. Don't mind, she said, he can be between us. The phone. Who in the name of God is calling at this hour of the night?

• 100

He was chalk white from messy hair to toes, no pink anywhere, so that the shallow definition of muscle in the chest, abdomen, and quadriceps seemed sculptural, a young Hermes by a sentimental follower of Thorvaldsen working in alabaster. The eyes were open and blank, the mouth peaceful. Both hands were curled as if in anxious preparation for catching some object about to fall. A student of yours? the policeman asked. He had a letter from you in his jeans pocket, wadded up. That's why we called you. Last session, Hugo said, at NFS Grundtvig, day student, lived on the warehouse end of Kalksten. He'd dropped out of school. Cocaine, the policeman said, OD. They're doing it all over the world, and why? I don't know, Hugo said, needing to cry but knowing that he couldn't. Do you?

Les Exploits de Nat Pinkerton de Jour en Jour: Un Texte de René Magritte Translated and Improved

Nat Pinkerton, the private detective, has arrived by horsecar, foot, and elevator at his office in New York. As soon as he has handed his bowler, gloves, and cane to the buttons, his lieutenant introduces a client.

— My case, the client, who is a lady of the upper middle class, explains without preamble, is one the likes of which you have never heard. My husband plays the bassoon in the Nineteenth Precinct Fireman's Marching Band. Our cook is Irish. I have a weakness for the finer things.

Nat Pinkerton lights a cheroot, listens attentively, makes a note with a pencil from time to time.

— I see it all, he says.

— The potato stew, she says, was strewn, you understand, from the living-room linoleum to the fire escape.

— You had no premonition? You suspected nothing?

— The tureen shattered in countless pieces right before my eyes.

She leaves. The detective gives orders to his lieutenant. The lieutenant, disguised as a Wall Street broker, leaves with a shotgun and bloodhound.

The detective writes a letter. He affixes a pink postage stamp depicting General George Washington, value three centimes. He uses a pseudonym in his return address.

He admires his office. A portrait of Mozart hangs above the steam radiator. On a table covered with a turkey carpet there is an Edison phonograph, an electric fan, a porcelain bust mapped phrenologically, a stereopticon viewer, a revolver, a lantern, an Argand astral lamp.

Towards noon, his morning's work being over, he strolls down Broadway to a well-appointed restaurant. He has an andouillette, some salad, and a half bottle of sauterne. He takes his coffee on the terrace, where he makes notes in a small book.

After his meal, he takes his customary walk. From habit he makes a mental photograph of all the people he passes. Everybody, he knows, is a potential criminal. The avenues are an endless spectacle. Indians from the Plains, trappers from Canada, English tourists easily spotted by their monocles and rolled umbrellas, senators from the capital who have Negro servants carrying their law books and writs, actresses of unsurpassed beauty lolling in carriages, John Jacob Astor looking out the window of his mansion.

He notices that his client of the morning is sitting in Central Park.

He penetrates the disguise of a well-known anarchist who is trying to pass for a nursemaid wheeling a pram. He steps deftly across the street, blowing his police whistle while felling the anarchist with one stroke of his powerful arm.

— Desist, Sir, cries a policeman arriving on the scene. You cannot strike a respectable nursemaid on the avenues of New York!

— Fool! says Nat Pinkerton. Do you not see that this is Osip Przwynsczki, the notorious anarchist from Paris, France?

Lifting the baby from its pram, he strips it to show that in effect it is a bundle of dynamite sticks bound with a fuse.

Soon after he goes into a bookstore to select a volume for his afternoon's reading. He chooses Captain Wilkes's *Voyages*.

Twice on the way back to his office he is shot at by dastardly outlaws whose careers he has thwarted. As always, they miss. The detective frequently consults the mirror in his hat to see who is behind him. At his tobacconist he buys a box of John Ruskin cigars and the latest edition of the *Herald Tribune*.

At the corner of Forty-Second Street and the Avenue Christophe-Colombe one of his operatives dressed as a banjo player from the Louisiana Purchase breaks into a tap dance, singing *Love Them Watermelons Mighty Fine* while reporting *sotto voce* and out of the side of his mouth that a slayer of six with ax for whom the Metropolitan Police have looked in vain is across the street buying an eggplant and some endives.

The detective nips over, coshes the criminal, and blows his whistle.

— Do I have to do all your work for you? he says tauntingly to the squadron of policemen who gallop up in a Black Maria.

Back in his office, he lights a cigar and reads his book. The lieutenant arrives and reads his report from scraps of paper secreted about his person. Nat Pinkerton files the information away in his unfailing memory, like wax to receive, like marble to retain.

The buttons bring him a telegram on a salver.

— Just as I thought! he says, telegram in hand.

Two women are presented by the lieutenant, and as soon as they have outlined their case, they weep awhile before leaving.

— Why, Nat Pinkerton asks his lieutenant, are matters so transparent to me, so opaque to everybody else?

The lieutenant does not answer, but smiles knowingly.

Nat Pinkerton reads about Captain Wilkes's antarctic expedition with genuine appreciation. He would like to see a penguin walking about upright and gabbling. He would like to hear the piercing cry of the albatross.

The door flies open and there, suddenly, is Florent Carton Dalton, leader of the famous gang. Though he wears a bandana across his face just under the eyes, Nat Pinkerton recognizes him and laughs at him while snapping his finger under his nose.

— Your time has come, you rancid son of a bitch! cries F. C. Dalton.

— Yours first! replies Nat Pinkerton, drawing a revolver from a holster concealed inside his coat and shooting Dalton then and there.

At eventide the lieutenant makes an arrest. One of the lady clients of the afternoon, he ascertained, was living with an acrobat as his concubine. Together they received stolen goods. The lieutenant is now free to return to his boardinghouse, his day's work well done. But not before he makes his report to Nat Pinkerton, whose thoughtful eyes register the interest he takes in the matter. The report is recorded in shorthand by a secretary and placed in the detective's files.

Then Nat Pinkerton goes home for the day. He stops at a quiet brasserie for a game of cards with his friends and a drink before dinner. Even here he knows the weaver by his tooth and the compositor by his thumb, the carpenter by his saw and hammer and the prostitute by her leer and the spots on her face.

He is withal a kindly soul, Nat Pinkerton, and buys a pretzel for the dog of the brasserie. By nine-thirty he is home. His wife and mother-in-law have waited for him in the dining room and together they eat some meat and vegetables. The detective is silent about his day's work. Instead, he gives his whole attention to his wife and mother-in-law. They are actresses and he has promised to write them a play fitted to their talents. His mother-in-law fancies aristocratic roles from the days before the Revolution. His wife favors a part in which she can cry and wring her hands, preferably in a scene with a cavalry officer of dashing appearance.

They all have a glass of Vichy water before bedtime. Nat Pinkerton, as always, goes down to check with the concierge that all the doors and windows are secured for the night.

He kisses his wife and mother-in-law, and goes off to his private bedroom. By a single candle he records some memoranda, to study some effective author's style for felicities of phrasing and purity of diction with an eye to writing down some of his more curious exploits which not many, but a discerning few, must surely find worthy of intelligent attention. *Secundo*, to recommence Sandow's exercises for toning the muscles and slimming the waist. *Tertio*, to purchase the new patented flyswatter as advertised in the evening paper, as a modern adjunct for his office.

The Jules Verne Steam Balloon

• KING OF PRUSSIA I IN D MAJOR, K. 575

Summer morning, awake a tick before the clock's ring, the work of bird-charm and circadian wheels, Hugo Tvemunding, assistant classics master and gym instructor at NFS Grundtvig, Troop Commander of Spejderkorps 235, and doctoral candidate in Theology, sat bolt upright in bed to yawn and stretch. The Great Walrus, said Mariana beside him, her eyes still closed, is on the loose, grumping all rivals away from his rocks. His walruser is reared up like a gander trying to see over the hedge, but first we must say our prayers. Hugo recited the prayer to the creator of being that he'd said every morning since he was a very little boy, a prayer composed by his pastor father. Amen, said Mariana. Franklin has slept through it all. Have not, said Franklin. Amen, too. Tickle me, and I'll bite. My rocks, said Hugo. Franklin for all his contribution to the dialogue is still asleep. Long hairy feet on the floor, said Mariana, who wore a shirt of Hugo's for a nightgown, square pinktoed feet on the floor, shapely girl's feet on the floor, plop, slap, and gracefully silent. Who lost a Band-Aid in the bed? Your T-shirt fits Franklin like a potato sack on a weasel.

• HOLLYHOCKS

Hugo's run before breakfast was along a macadam road through pine-woods with an undergrowth of fern and laurel. He freed himself with every stride of the residue of dreams, of warm lethargies that had nested in his muscles, of anxieties that had made trash in his mind. He spoke to rabbits hopping across the road, to a cheeky fox doing a little dance in a clearing. The light was silver, early, cold. He had dreamed of his mother standing beside hollyhocks and coleus. Idiotically, he had said, *They're dead, aren't they?* She'd said, with her usual placid composure, *Why no, dear, they're not dead.* And indeed nothing could have been more alive than these dream hollyhocks and coleus, so crisply beautiful in the accurate light of the dream. And his mother's kindly ghost was like a blessing. She wore her apron, as for housework, and her voice was as sweet as springwater. White latticework of the back porch door behind her. A perfectly temperate summer day. *Why no, dear, they're not dead at all.*

• CABIN WITH SKYLIGHT

Stables once, Hugo's room was designed and appointed by a drawing master who, having made it into a Danish Modern oblong of continuous space with a skylight, left to take a position elsewhere. Bed and worktable under the skylight, bookcases, chairs beyond, toward the kitchen area, which had a small barn window over the sink and cabinets. On the walls were a large photograph of Bourdelle's *Herakles the Archer*, a Mondriaan of the severest geometric period, a Paul Klee angel grinning about some sacred mischief, a photograph of Brancusi's *Torso d'un jeune homme*, and three paintings by Hugo: Mariana naked, slouched reading in a chair, a still life of meadow flowers in a coffee mug, and a large painting that had once been of the Bicycle Rider, repainted with Tom Agernkop as model.

• GARDEN

The colors in the dream where his mother stood placidly in her coverall, print cotton polka-dot gloves, and straw hat were those of photographs in *The Country Garden* and *House and Family*: early greens, soft browns, reticent blues in sharp silvery focus.

• WATER

This is Franklin the Rabbit Who Invented Electricity, Hugo said to Rutger, Kim, Asgar, Tom, and Anders in the showers. We've run six kilometers, Franklin said. Oof! These wolfcub mystery knots you did my laces in, Hugo, won't untie. *Hugo!* Knowing eyes found laughing eyes. Let me, Rutger said, kneeling. Franklin, looking hard at Kim and Anders under a shower together, soaping each other, wiggled his fingers at his ears and ruckled like a dove. They like each other, Skipper, Hugo said.

• WHEAT

He wasn't out to set himself up through signs and wonders, Hugo said to his Sunday School class. He was not concerned about who he was. That showed in everything he did. And from moment to moment he was the people he suffered with, whom he could cure or comfort or free. Most of these are people estranged from themselves by pain or deformity. People who are out of their minds are no good to anybody else, and Yeshua's idea of man was that he was first of all someone who could help another.

• EYES BLUE WITH FATE

A nipper, Mariana sighed, locked herself in the laundry room and no amount of cajoling and instructions about the catch did anything but make her howl the louder, so I had to climb onto the roof and jimmy open a window the size of a handkerchief and plead with the little demon to listen while I showed her how to let herself out, and another nipper stuck modelling clay up his nose and turned blue, and another had hiccups for an hour, and another was passing around color photos of her big brother doing it with his girl on the sunroom floor, and another barfed on the vocabulary cards. So I've had it, and want love, understanding, and sour cream pineapple pancakes for supper. She was holding an ice cube to Franklin's knee, which was skinned bloody. His silkflop thatch had leaftrash and twigs in it. A smutch of mud saddled his nose. The seat of his pants was piped with clay. They had all converged at the bus stop, Franklin from the soccer field, Mariana off the bus, and Hugo from class, going home. While Mariana set up a field hospital to deal with Franklin, Hugo, out of his jeans, exiguous briefs taxed by a randy flex, said that he would provide love, Franklin understanding, and Mariana sour cream pineapple pancakes. Iodine, Mariana ordered, and fill the sink with hot soapy water, skin Franklin of his pants and underpants and put the one in the other. The two in the other, Franklin said. Hugo is hanging out like the donkeys at the zoo. Better still, Mariana said, strip the lout and stand him in the sink, soap him up, and pour panfuls of water over his head. Family life is wonderfully exciting, Hugo said, lifting Franklin into the sink. You know Pascal? he asked. I know Pascal, Hugo said. He is the light of Holger Sigurjonsson's life, as everybody from the kitchen staff to the headmaster knows. He, said Franklin around the washcloth, lost one of his shoes. So I told him to throw the other away. What good is one shoe? They tease him real pitiful about hr. Sigurjonsson, so we beat up Otto with the weasel eyes. He was picking on Pascal. I heard him. I didn't know, Hugo said, that you were friends with Pascal. I am now, Franklin said. After we beat up Otto. Well yes, Hugo said, let's hear about that. I booted him in the butt, Franklin said, hard. He called Pascal a name, and Pascal just took it. I was behind them both, you see, and here was Otto's butt for the kicking. That's when he tried to pin me, and I did my knee there. I'm not listening, Mariana said, I'm not hearing a word of this. So, said Franklin, Pascal got in it then. He pushed Otto on a shoulder while hooking his ankle: laid him flat. Then we both jumped on him. Hr. Sigurjonsson showed Pascal how to defend himself.

• YESHUA IN THE WHEAT

Goose grass, said Hugo, found with knotweed in hard ground poor soil cinder paths. Old meadows are thick with it, an archaic wheat from which the horseriding plunderers made bread and foddered their shaggy Shetlands. It came to Eleusis, Joseph Gaertner thought, by way of India. That's why he named it *Eleusine indica*. Crabgrass and crowfoot are of the same family. The florets are ashlared thick along the spikes, see? And there's no awn. Grass, Franklin said, is just grass. Here, said Mariana, is where we get Hugo's handsome blond cross-eyed stare. Meaning I hear it but I don't believe it. The pathfinders never get it, only us, and the occasional Grundtvigger. Franklin calm and unheeding. What Mariana says is what Mariana says. It has nothing to do with him until she starts shouting. Emmer of the prophets embedded in the clay of Ugaritic pots under the botanist's microscope is like implicit information in a text. It came along, like Franklin underfoot, of itself. Now I'm grass, Franklin said.

• ACORN IN ITS CUP

To get to the bus stop where Mariana with shining eyes and bright smile arrived at afternoon's end, Hugo damp from his second gym class, his book bag charged with Latin and Greek exercises to correct, had but to cross the soccer field and amble along two blocks of guardedly prosperous houses with colorful gardens behind low front walls. If he let the class go ten minutes early and skipped a shower, he had time to walk to the bus stop by way of the meadow beyond the wood where he could sit under a favorite oak, elbows on knees, and have a rich moment of calm and anticipation. The river shone at the other side of the meadow, if the light was right. Here passages of the thesis on Yeshua took form and texture, the day disclosed patterns, abrasions healed, letters were opened and read.

Papa's hollyhocks. Papa's reading, the lectures and concerts he had been to. A note on a Hebrew word.

Aakjaer Minor had begun a cataleptic syndrome that was as yet more comic than serious. He hugged people and wouldn't, or couldn't, let go. In the locker room he'd seen Golo Hansen embarrassed and helpless in Alexander Aakjaer's grasp. I don't want to hurt him, Golo had wailed to Hugo. He grabs people like this, his eyes go blank, and he won't turn loose. Hugo had said, quit trying to pull him loose. Just stand cool. He got me the other day, Asgar said, and two people couldn't pry him off. It's mental. He doesn't know what you're talking about when it's over. Hugo had studied the unfocussed eyes, the sweaty back of the neck, cold wrists, locked knees and elbows. Gently he'd guided Golo out of Alexander's gripping arms, hoisted the suddenly slack Alexander onto his shoulders and carried him to the infirmary where he said to Nurse that Aakjaer Minor had had a dizzy spell in gym and only needed to lie still for a while. Nurse nevertheless stuck a thermometer in Alexander's mouth and took his pulse, seeing nothing interesting in either.

• JONAS

The pompion or million creeps upon the ground if nothing be by it whereon it may take hold and climb with very great ribbed rough and prickly branches whereon are set large rough leaves cut in on the edges with deep gashes and dented besides, with many claspers also, which wind about everything they meet. The flowers are great and large, hollow and yellow, divided at the brim into five parts, at the bottom of which grows the fruit sometimes of the bigness of a man's body and oftentimes less, in some ribbed or bunched, in others plain and either long or round, green or yellow. The seed is great flat and white, lying in the middle of the watery pulp. The root is of the bigness of a man's thumb, dispersed underground with many small fibers. They are boiled in fair water and salt, or in powdered beef broth, sometimes in milk, and so eaten, or else buttered. The seed, as well as of cowcumbers and melons, are cooling, and serve for emulsions in the like manner as almond milks, for those troubled with the stone.

• BLUE PUP TENT

In the ferns beyond birches. Hugo slowed, running in place, and hollered *ho!* Whoever you are, he sang in stentorian *buffo*, I come in peace. Silence. Brilliant early morning northern light. *Ho!* from the pup tent. I'll go away, Hugo said, if you want me to. This is school property. Grundtviggers are you? Tvemunding here, having a run before breakfast. A head, bare shoulders, an ironic sleepy grin. Anders. Out of the tent on knuckles and toes, mother naked. Morning, he said.

Through the birches, behind Anders, Quark on a silver wolf loping.

Kim and I, Anders said. Kim looked out, blond hair over his eyes. He crawled out monkey-nimble. A hug from Anders.

• RIVER

The divestment of Franklin in the meadow by the river. Mariana flourished a toy trumpet. The grasses, Hugo said, go from Tolland Man's gruel of flaxseed and goosegrass to Roman porridge, which was linseed roasted with barley and coriander, pounded in a mortar, salted, boiled, and served in a bowl to Horace dining with Virgil. Columella fancied it, and Pliny mentions the toothsomeness of rustic Tuscan porridge on a winter morning. Meadow with goats to gaze at as he ate. Like us, said Mariana, bleating and folding Franklin's togs. There were Iron Age grape pips at Donja Dolina. Bet they ate frogs, too, Mariana said, and green lizards. People upstream in a boat, Franklin said. Voices carry over water. Master Sigurjonsson and Pascal without a stitch. Ho, said Mariana. Pascal I mean, Franklin said, climbing Hugo to stand on his shoulders. Hr. Ess has on a cap, wristwatch, and little triangle underpants like Hugo's. Swim out, Hugo said, and climb aboard.

• OLD MIRRORS FLECKED AND TARNISHED

On a long walk that took him near the Nordkalksten seawall and warehouses, Hugo had seen the Bicycle Rider hefting his bike up the stone steps, swinging onto it in the road. Their eyes met, with no recognition in the Rider's, though he was already a day student at NFS Grundtvig but not yet someone Hugo had tried to be friendly toward. His jeans were unzipped, the pod of his dingy briefs pouching through. His eyes had been dead, as when Hugo had last seen them in the police morgue.

• ASTERS AND ZINNIAS

Papa in a folding hammock chair by his hollyhocks, straw boater over his eyes. Hugo's theology, he said, is of course his need to undo me. Not by cracking my head on a dusty road in Greece, but as an intelligent child takes its toys apart to see what makes them go. Ridiculous, but there you are. Papa, Hugo said, I know what makes you go. And the machinery is too fine for my fingers. I hope I'm something like. Peas in a pod, Mariana said, if you know what to look for. You have the same sense of house, of space, of time. You eat alike. I didn't know how to take a walk until Hugo annexed me. Or how a room can be the whole world. It's awful, Franklin said, but it's fun. Tell me, Pastor Tvemunding said from under his hat, holding out an arm to invite Franklin over. Franklin came, got hugged, and climbed astride. Papa, Hugo said, keeps his hat over his eyes so as not to look at Franklin snake naked. How modern I'm willing to be, Papa said, is, I see, still a matter for doubt. Notice everything, Franklin said. Know where everything comes from, a hundred years back.

• ANEMONE

Matter, the physicists seem to be saying, was not stuff before creation: critical tensions in nothingness, the universal vacuum, became so energetic that they exploded. Critical tensions? Papa asked. Force, said Hugo. The only thing the physicists can reach back to is a great force present in all matter and space. Well then, Papa said, scattering leaves with his stick, there's God. As they see Him. If, Hugo said, man in God's image was Adam, God in man's image was Yeshua. If matter was not stuff before creation, then God can be a pattern of energy rather than an oxygen breather and processor of carbohydrates. That we are in His image then means that He is and we are animations of the same energy system. Except, perhaps, His anima occupies the whole sea of neutrinos that is boundless but limited, and we each occupy bodies only, energy systems that are bounded but limitless, exchanging love and conversation, procreating both bodies and minds. God's procreation is continuous, ours occasional. Yeshua is an occasional aspect of a continuity.

• BREAKFAST

Franklin. Hair carrot and brass. Irides seagreen, pupils hyacinth. Pathfinder brogans, collapsed socks. Lots of practical irony and cautious reticence, the hippety-hop who invented electricity. Love me some geography, he says to the mush bowl, because a map is a jigsaw puzzle. What I like is where the driblet islands make a trail at the south poke of things, left behind, all on a drift to the west. And to the north, crumbly islands. Love islands. Show him the inland island in France, bounded by four rivers. Plains islands bounded by mountains. A country, then, he opines, is a lot of people pretending they're an island, because they all speak the same language. Well, sometimes. Or because they have a common interest, like the Swiss. There is no place without time, no time without place. So, says Franklin, knuckling his nose, you can't say where without saying when. The Mediterranean when it had seals in it. Holland before tulips. Everything wanders, he says. Land, people, animals, trees.

• OUT FROM JOPPA

Two ways, Hugo said, and Papa cocked his head to listen. Like John, as in eleven Matthaeus, neither eating nor drinking, and the opinion of the public is that you are owned and operated by a devil, or like Yeshua, eating and drinking, and the people say here's a glutton and a drunkard, the friend of tax collectors and sinners. And, Papa said, that's yet another logion where the sign of Jonas is the pivot. The vine is to be judged by its gourd.

• DOVE

By wholeness of being.

• FIG

Neutrino here, Hugo said, our Franklin, is as yet all luck. Whenever the angel rings the silver run in a sound of trumpets, he thrusts his sickle in, the wheat topples in a golden rush, the chaff dances in the air, and the harvest song is the only one his red tongue knows morning noon and night. Whereas those of us who shave and pay taxes always seem to get in line at the post office behind an Oriental trying to mail a live chicken to Sri Lanka. Look at McTaggart the English master. He loses his car habitually in the parking lot. That his disciples in Transcendental Meditation and Buddhist raising of the consciousness are all feebleminded hankerers who will clot around any mountebank he does not notice. He walks across flower beds puffing the beauties of nature to one of his morons. He was the only one of the faculty the Bicycle Rider esteemed and thought a bright teacher. To blow like a dead leaf in the wind, irresponsible, irresponsive. Which beautiful teaching, Mariana said, laid the Bicycle Rider out on the slab at the police morgue.

• MONKEYS AND PARROTS

If, Mariana read to Franklin lying on the carpet and rolling a soccer ball inchmeal from crotch to chin, the forest were darker it did not seem to be more silent. They could hear a kind of buzzing in the treetops, a vague noise coming from the branches. Looking upwards, the three men could see indistinctly something like a great platform stretched out some forty meters above the ground. There must be at that height a tremendous entanglement of branches without any cranny through which the daylight could pierce. A thatched roof would not have been more lightproof. This explained the darkness that prevailed beneath the trees. Where they had camped that night the nature of the ground had changed greatly. No more intermingled branches or brambles, no more of those thorns that had kept them from leaving the footpath. A scanty grass, like a prairie that neither rain nor spring ever watered. The trees, at intervals from seven to ten meters, resembled pillars supporting some colossal edifice, and their branches must cover an area of several thousand hectares. There were masses of African sycamores whose trunks were formed of a number of stems firmly united toward the ground, bob bobs. Baobabs, Hugo said from his desk, a majestic great gray-green tree that huddles its trunks like celery. Bob bobs, read Mariana, recognizable by the gourdlike shape of their bole, with a circumference of seven to ten meters and surmounted by an enormous mass of hanging branches. There were silk cotton trees with their trunks opening into a series of hollows big enough for a man to hide in. Mahogany trees with trunks a meter and a half in diameter from which might have been excavated dugout canoes from five to seven meters long. Ho, Hugo said, Zuntz on the centurion with Jules Verne from across the room has filled me with lovingkindness, especially as Monsieur Verne's expositor has had her hand inside her knickers from the beginning of the chapter. Can I help it if I'm a sweet person? she said. When, Franklin said, twirling the soccer ball on his chin, I get to my peter, it jumps. See? Chin to peter, peter to chin. Phenomenal! Hugo said. I'll bet if you went to the baker's, by way of the kiosk for an evening paper, you might find a half dozen strawberry-jam cakes with custard topping that we can have with coffee, which I'll make, as Mariana is not going to be able to see straight after our expression, or expressions, of mutual esteem.

• BLUE SUMMER SKY

Hugo under his oak at the meadow's edge saw the oval shadow of the hot-air balloon sliding toward him before he looked up and saw the balloon itself, a gaudy upside-down pear shape the oiled silk of which was zoned in bands: the equatorial one was a rusty persimmon, a Mongol color, and around it were the figures of the zodiac copied from the mosaic floor of Bet Alpha Synagogue in Byzantine Israel, archaic but supple of line. The band above was bells and pomegranates in orange and blue, the one below was egg-and-dart Hellenistic. The basket was of wicker and belonged to the protomachine age, for a propeller that seemed to be made of four cricket bats was turned by a fanbelt connected to a brass cylinder leaking steam vapor. There was a wooden rudder, and levers at the taffrail. Three ten-year-old boys were the crew, as happy as grigs at their work bringing the balloon down right in front of Hugo, who stood and gaped, at a loss to account for anything he was seeing. The boys were dressed in nautical Scandinavian togs, with long scarves around their necks, as if the air from which they'd descended was very cold. One boy manipulated a lever that seemed to bring the balloon down, another braked the propeller, which stopped spinning and rolled to a lazy halt. Puffs of vapor smoked from the cylinder. The boys' bright grins were for the joy of surprising Hugo, for the joy of being aeronauts in a balloon on a fine summer day, and for the joy of being messengers, which they said they were, talking all at once. Who in the name of God are you? Hugo asked. Where have you come from? My name is Tumble, and my friends are Quark and Buckeye. Where we come from we're not to say, and we're messengers. Bringing a message, Quark said helpfully. The coordinates are right, Buckeye said, consulting a length of paper between two rollers. Oak tree, meadow, island, Denmark. Hugo Tvemunding by way of worldly name. Shapes alphabet into words about the Company. *Yeryüzü kendi kendine bir toprak.* Buckeye! Tumble said sweetly, you're off band: that's Turkish. Sorry, said Buckeye, I was about to blush anyway, this part of the printout about shepherd to the young, a good son, and superb lover in both flesh and spirit, *tam avidus quam taurus* in a different hand in the margin, the dispatcher I suppose. *Nesuprantamas disonansas tarp*, oops! sor-ree. Anyway, you're the right soul. Yes, said Tumble, and here's the message. Road auspicious. Though young, act like a man. Be steadfast, patient, and silent.

Why? Hugo asked. About what?

That, smiled Quark, we are not free to say.

• BOUNDARY

There is only one sense: touch. The sun, by way of caroming off a mellow brick wall with lonely afternoon light on it, firm plump pair of breasts with

delectable nipples, a page of Homer, touches the eyes. Eating is touch carried
to the utmost. Vibrant air touches the ear. Smell is so many particles from
aromatic things. The world is a mush of matter rather than the separateness
we ascribe to things. Franklin in his Wolf Cub cricket cap, blue shirt with
yellow kerchief, little blue pants, tall ribbed socks, and red sneakers listened
to Hugo in Eagle Scout khakis with solemn attention. Boys named Abel and
Bruno had got out of him, moments before the powwow, that he has no
father, that his sister Mariana is the bedmate of Scoutmaster Tvemunding,
that he has only been camping with Hugo and Mariana, that he is poor, that
Hugo makes love to Mariana lots and lots, and that his uniform is so new
it has little squares of paper in all the pockets with an inspector's number,
to accompany complaint of manufacturing defect. As to other questions,
Franklin had offered to bloody Bruno's nose for him. Knots, naming of tent
parts and tools, cards with animal tracks, cards with flowers and weeds, and
here was Scoutmaster Tvemunding, who taught Latin, Greek, and gym at
NFS Grundtvig and Sunday School at Treenigheden, talking about everything being touch. Eugenius, he said, front and forward. Theodor, front and
forward. Face each other, tall and straight, shoulders back. Theodor, cup
your hands. Eugenius is going to give you something, out of his wild imagination, and you are going to feel it, in your wild imagination, and describe
it, how it feels. A frog! Eugenius said. Well, said Theodor, I had a frog in my
hands just the other day, and a snake, and a hedgehog, so I'm not up a creek.
A frog looks damp but is dry, looks flabby but is hard. It twitches, trying to
jump away, but can be still, probably because it's scared. I'd be scared. It's
cool. Its throat pulses.

• ZUM ZIELE FÜHRT DICH DIESE BAHN

Theodor, Hugo said, didn't know the dative of accommodation from a rat's
ass and has been stricken with amnesia in the matter of ablative absolutes,
Frits and Asgar bloodied each other in a fight back of the gym, nasty little
beasts, the stupidly inconsiderate grounds trolls ran a power mower just outside the windows for half of Greek, and around three Ulrich gave me a frantic
signal in gym to come quick. Golo and Abel were, for reasons best known
to themselves, having a little conviviality outside study hall, where they were
supposed to be, playing push and pull with each other's pizzles while gazing

into each other's big soulful eyes I suppose, fine by me and nobody could care less though they have rooms and showers and woods and meadows in which to welcome puberty until they're cross-eyed and gasping for breath, but why waste the ten minutes before study hall, and then Aakjaer Minor, who grabs people and goes cataleptic, happens along and pins them both. Ulrich was the first to notice this predicament, and knowing that McTaggart had study hall and would be stomping along crabwise at any moment, and would bore everybody for days with the psychology of it all, had the diplomatic genius to push all three into the broom closet and sprint for the gym. We nipped back. McTaggart was bleating about combining study with transcendental meditation, so we could craftily open the broom closet and walk the interlocked three down the hall, one walking backward and zipping himself up, the other sideways, and both carrying the clinging Aakjaer with my and Ulrich's help, God laughing at us all fit to kill. We disentangled the mass in my office. Abel, who had not managed to get his britches up with his arms pinned to his sides, stood there in pretty outrage. What in hell does it mean? he begged of me.

Mariana, listening with wide eyes, had deshoed and unsocked Hugo as he talked in the chair where he had flopped and sagged, tugged his trousers off, and was unbuttoning his shirt when a banging on the door announced Franklin in full Cub Scout fig. O Lord, Hugo sighed, I was forgetting that tonight's the little bastards in yellow and blue, with beanies. Hi, said Franklin. Things look real interesting. Hugo, Mariana said, has had a trying day, and has taken a full ten minutes to get over it.

• ZWECK

In pipestem trews snug of cleft, flat Dutch cap, thickwove jersey, Norfolk jacket, hobnailed brogues, and Finnish scarf with an archaic pattern of reindeer and runes worked into its weave, Tumble climbed from the basket of the steam balloon, bounced from his jump, and cued Quark and Buckeye, poised with flute and glockenspiel, to give him a tune. *Master Erastus*, he sang, stomping with seesawing shoulders and chiming smile, *Equuleus quagga!* Likes, said Quark in recitative over the catch, clover bluegrass dill, spring onions oats and hay. Kin to, said Buckeye, lowering his flute, Eohippus Five Toes, silver wolves, red deer on Rum, dandelions, and Ertha when she's broody. Maybe, said Quark, depressing the declinator, which seeped vapor, but the mykla puts them in with asses burros zebras and horses of the good old Hwang Ho Valley, don't it? Yuss, said Tumble, but Buckeye means chord. Spartan spadgers, springbokker, leapers and runners. So hold fast, wait long, and don't speak. No, not to anybody.

• ARCHAIC TORSO OF APOLLO

Even though we can never see the head that sang, with its deer's eyes staring at infinity, we have the strong torso from whose animal grace we can imagine the hot summer clarity of its gaze. If the gone head is still not there, in light, why then does the proud chest disturb your looking, or the sweet shift of the hips, slight as a smile, that takes our eyes down the cunning body, to its cluster of seeds? Otherwise this stone would stand senseless under the polished slope of its shoulders, without its wild balance, and would not be as rich with light as the sky with stars. The world sees you, too. You must change your life.

• AN EVENT ALSO HAPPENS WHERE IT IS KNOWN

Out past the warehouses and quays on Nordkalksten is a seawall of gray stone. A catwalk at its base, a bicycle path along the top, with iron rail. Harbor, river, barges. Here one could see old men fishing, sailors sleeping off a terrible drunk, and sunbathers spread against the slant of the wall. Boys in dingy bargain-basement briefs, boys impudently naked.

• UNDER

We distinguish this seventh stratum by stringers of the stone that readily melts in fire of the second order. Beneath this is another ashy rock, light in weight and five foot thick. Next comes a lighter stratum the colors of ash and a foot thick. Beneath this lies the eleventh stratum, dark and like the seventh, two foot through. Below the last is a twelfth stratum, soft and of a whitish color, two foot thick. The weight of this sits on the thirteenth stratum, ashy and a foot thick, whose weight in turn is supported by a fourteenth stratum of black color. There follows this another black stratum half a foot thick, which is again followed by a sixteenth stratum still blacker in color, whose thickness is also the same. Beneath this, and last of all, lies the cupriferous stratum, black colored and schistose, in which there sometimes glitter scales of gold-colored pyrites in very thin sheets, which, as I have said elsewhere, often take the forms of various living things.

• HOLLYHOCKS ALONG A GARDEN WALL

I'm wonderfully delighted, Pastor Tvemunding said to Mariana, that you and Hugo are friends. He has always been a friendly boy. He used to toddle off behind the postman, and grieve that he could not stay longer than to hand over the mail and exchange comments on the weather. He made friends with the girl who delivered butter and eggs. He fell in love with all his schoolmates. He is indeed, Mariana said, a very loving person. His loving nature, Pastor Tvemunding said, causes him grief from time to time. You know about the student whom he calls the Bicycle Rider?

Who's dead, Mariana. I know what you mean. He hurt Hugo.

Because, Pastor Tvemunding said, Hugo had never really before, I believe, encountered evil face to face. He doesn't want to admit that evil cannot be dealt with. He cannot believe that there are wholly selfish people drowned in themselves, beyond the reach of love and understanding. That there are people who, impotent to create, destroy. That there are people whose self-loathing is so deep they know nothing of generosity and invariably do the mean thing even when they might as easily do the generous one. The young man was on drugs, and had been for years, but I'm not one to blame drugs for human evil: the evil is there before the drugs, which are part of the meanness and not its cause.

All this theological work, which will not take him into the ministry, began with a remark I made years ago, that God will remain inscrutable and uncertain forever, but that Jesus—Hugo's Yeshua, for the Aramaic name is of the essence for him—had an intuitive idea of God that put goodness in our hands. He is light, of which we are free to partake, or be in darkness. We can be transparent to our fellow man, or opaque.

• BUCKEYE

Possum ate a lightning bug and now he shines inside.

• RED AND YELLOW ZINNIAS

I want to be up-to-date, Pastor Tvemunding said at tea, reaching over to wipe whipped cream from the corners of Franklin's mouth with his napkin. There's Hugo's room, and the guest room which is so jolly with the apple tree at the window. Mariana and I, Hugo said, will sleep together, and I'll rig out my old scout cot for Franklin. But, said the pastor, there's the guest room for him. Oh no, Hugo said, travellers should stay together.

• MEADOW WITH GOLDFLOWERS AND POPPIES

Buckeye in a Portuguese sailor's shirt, abrupt white denim pants, beret, and espadrilles climbed backward down the rope ladder of the balloon, singing *onward under over through!* Quark tossed the anchor onto the meadow. The balloon tilted in its drift, exhaled vapor from its cylinders, bounced and swayed as Tumble pumped the declinators. Quark swung himself over the wicker taffrail with a deft scissor kick and landed springing. Tumble closed valves, cinched a line, made an entry in a ledger and vaulted out, rolling forward in a somersault. Ho! said Buckeye, Hi! said Quark, Hup! said Tumble. *For adoration beyond match*, sang Tumble pulling his sailor's middy over his blond rick of windscrumpled hair, *the scholar bulfinch aims to catch. The soft flute's ivory touch*, sang Quark sopranino, his gray American sweatshirt halfway over his head. *And, careless on the hazel spray*, Buckeye sang as he snatched off his Portuguese sailor's blouse, *the daring redbreast keeps at bay the damsel's greedy clutch*. Shoeless, sockless, Tumble backed out of his sailor's pants singing, *While Israel sits beneath his fig. With coral root and amber spring*, Quark sang with trills and a cadenza as he wriggled off his Sears Roebuck blue jeans. *The weaned adventurer sports*, tossing his short white pants into the gondola of the balloon. Tumble, pretending to blush, thumbed down his drawers, Quark and Buckeye pindling briefs, and the three in their pinkbrown slender ribby nakedness sang in chiming Mozartian harmony, *Where to the palm the jasmin cleaves for adoration mongst the leaves the gale his peace reports. Now labor*, they sang, making a triangle of arms on one another's shoulders, *his reward receives, for adoration counts his sheaves, to peace, her bounteous prince. The nectarine his strong tint imbibes, and apples of ten thousand tribes, and quick peculiar quince.*

• TROLLFLÖJTEN

Ring-tailed kinkajous trotting on the logging road, bouncing and siffling, squeaking and hopping, in pairs and trios, alone and in quartets. Yellow parrots above them, monkeys and kingfishers. Franklin's world, Mariana said. Years ago he was a rat in the Pied Piper festival, he and scads of littles in brown and gray rat suits with rope tails, creeping along behind the Piper playing Mozart. I remember a rat who lost his way and had to be carried by a woman and restored to the pack. Wasn't me, Franklin said. I crept good.

• GOLDEN SAMPHIRE

Buckeye in the meadow, where the balloon was tethered. Tumble and Quark were leapfrogging by the river. He held out his hand for a meadowlark to fly to him and stand on his palm. She spoke to him. He answered in quail. Silly! she said. Do I look like a quail hen? He spoke goat. She laughed. Frog. Giggle.

• AURIGA. BETELGEUSE. BARNARD'S STAR.

In spite of their intangibility, neutrinos enjoy a status unmatched by any other known particle, for they are actually the most common objects in the universe, outnumbering electrons by a thousand million to one. In fact, the universe is really a sea of neutrinos, punctuated only rarely by impurities such as atoms. It is even possible that neutrinos collectively outweigh the stars, and therefore dominate the gravity of the cosmos.

• RIGHT THE SECOND TIME

Tom'll be here in a bit, Hugo said to Mariana nose to nose. I think I can walk, Mariana said, though my brains are all gone, so much jelly they are. There's somebody. It was Franklin. O wow, he said, looking squiggle-eyed and pretending to barf. Who, said Mariana, pulled his piddler till his eyes rolled back in his head the whole week we were at Papa Tvemunding's, while we had to make do with teenage smooching? You said Augustus would spoil me, Franklin said solemnly. I like Augustus. I imagine so, Hugo said. Nasty little spy. Papa with a dry cough to introduce the subject, which amused him tremendously, said that Franklin confided in him that we were not making love, but only kissing a lot and whispering, before we went to sleep. I guess, he'd opined, you wouldn't like them to, but he didn't tell us that Papa had laughed and said that love was a joyful and good thing, and that young people were very close to God when they made love. Franklin, being Franklin, next got Papa to say a good word for rabbity-nosed boys jacking off, in moderation, naturally. It's nature, Franklin said. To be thought of as fun. That was the afternoon the rascal so coolly shed his pants and stomped around upstairs whacking away. Afternoons, and once a morning and twice in the afternoon, Franklin explained, was because Augustus said I was to, but at night was because you said I was to, if I wanted. So I did. I suppose, Mariana said to the skylight, if a third party had assured him of the naturalness of the kinship between boys and monkeys, Franklin would have had no time to eat, sleep, or have all those long talks with Papa Tvemunding. Who, said Hugo, spoiled him rotten. I promised to write him a letter, Franklin said. I will, too. Tom's here, Mariana said.

Hugo, who had pulled on long sweatpants and a singlet and was howling for coffee, set the painting of the Bicycle Rider on the easel. He had whited out the lazily handsome blond face and its dead blue eyes. The right arm, on the fist of which the head had leaned, was also overpainted. Dark background's going, too, Hugo mused: it wants to be white. Mariana, her breasts loose under a rich blue pullover, was zipping herself into tight coral shorts when big Tom, tossing his floppy hair out of his eyes, shifted from foot to foot. He crossed his hands on his behind, touching a lampshade with an elbow. He then cupped them over his crotch, seeing instantly that, expand or contract, he was equally awkward. He tried sliding his fingers into his pockets, hitting the lampshade again, and settled for knuckling his nose and scratching a convenient itch on his thigh. Shown the painting, he stared at it. That, Hugo said, was that dopey kid who was a day student, the one who floated around on lysergic acid and managed the ultimate in trendy distance by killing himself with an overdose of God knows what. I tried getting his head out of his ass. I failed. No, Mariana said, he failed you.

Anyway, Hugo said, I'm going to repaint. Tom hates coffee, Mariana said brightly. Every time he's been here, he has suffered and squirmed. Beer, milk, fizz water, which? Beer, Tom said, his voice rasping at his own audacity. Head turned slightly, so that you're looking at me out of the side of your eyes. Right elbow on the chair arm. Everything else the same, except that your body is harder and better muscled than the Rider's, so I have all sorts of changes to make. Take off your pants. This sloshed Tom's beer. Leave your briefs on. They're nicely stinted and stressed.

The balloon, Hugo could see through the skylight, was just outside. He had learned on a walk with Mariana that she could not see Buckeye, Quark, and Tumble. They had come and stood gravely interested around while they sat under the oak, Mariana's head in Hugo's lap.

Burnt sienna, Hugo said, raw sienna, titanium white. Franklin made a great show of finding the tubes and laying them on the little table that served as a palette.

Buckeye was on the skylight, peering in. Short khaki pants, gray white and ochre striped soccer jersey, and not till he came into the room, through the door, in less time than the blinking of an eye, could you see his dinky blue cap.

Calabash! he said to Hugo, straked gourd pumpkin vine!

If I had some paper and a pencil and an envelope and a stamp, Franklin said, I could write Augustus. And, Mariana said, if you could spell and write so that anybody but God could read it. Put in your letter, Hugo said, that while we visited I saw what I needed to see. Say that the casting out of demons is the hub on which everything else turns. He'll know what I mean. The self is the demon. Demon out, daimon in.

O wow! Franklin said. Start spelling. Hugo painted, Tom, with only his good nature to see him through his ordeal, took courage from the fact that it was his beauty that got him into this, and thought of seducing Franklin without breaking Lemuel's heart, share him perhaps, and Mariana, and even Hugo, and the green-eyed sailor with the silver eyelashes, humped pectorals, and a sleepy friendly smile. Mariana spelled, Franklin wrote and erased and wrote again. Hugo painted.

Tumble was at the skylight, Quark looking over his shoulder. Why do you keep looking up? Mariana asked idly. The light, Hugo said. It's what I paint by.

Buckeye was inspecting Tom, closely, and with doggish curiosity. His eyes met Hugo's. Under all's a fire so fine it is and isn't in and out of time, a pulse of is, a pulse of isn't. But, Buckeye said with a shrug of his boney shoulders and a crinkle of dimples in his smile, that isn't worth knowing, is it? Over all's the nothing that's something because of the curving tides of the is and isn't. No matter, that, either. He stood behind Tom and put his hands around his neck and rested his chin in Tom's hair. Quark read Franklin's letter. Tumble sniffed Mariana. What matters, Buckeye said, is that there are so many who don't know their right hand from their left.

Jonah

In the harbor of Joppa in Phoenicia a merchant ship with two kids stitched in black on its sail the yellow of pumpkins was stowing and lashing its cargo when yet another passenger made his way through the crates of figs, bundles of cedarwood, and straw-bound casks of sweet water being unloaded from asses, to pay in full from a leather purse his fare to Tarshish.

He had a fine black beard, round as a basket. Though his carpetbags were neatly strapped and his clothes showed that he was an experienced traveler, there was a furtiveness in his eyes, as if there might be someone about whom he did not care to meet. His staff was of olive, and his name was Dove. *Teomim*, he read aloud the ship's name on the prow, so he was a man of letters. He added, by way of a friendly word with whoever might be interested, that for a sign of A Pair of Kids his people said Rebecca's Twins, or Esau and Yakov.

— Yes, said the captain, the good of pictures is that you can call them what you want. I have heard those stars called The Double Gazelle.

— Simeon and Levi also, Dove remarked.

The sea was as dark as wine, the sky sweet. A stout wind took them out of the bay, toward the other side of the world. A sailor played a tambourine, the sail swelled fat and tight, and the helmsman with a complacent bellow ordered sailors to let out or bring in lines, to trim this, and make that fast, until he was satisfied that his ship, the wind, and sea were in his hands.

— Grand weather! was the opinion of a merchant. While gourds are ripening and spiders spinning is the time to sail. This part of the year, I mean. Earlier, when swallows nest.

— Signs, said Dove, if we could but read them all.

— My guess, Brother Dove, is that your business in this world is with more than salt fish and dried figs?

— I'll wager a scholar, the captain said.

— A clerk, said Dove, in the survey service, but with some training in the scrolls.

He talked, as men of business talk, of his work with the boundary markers when the government extended the tax lands from the gates at Hamath to the shores of Arabah. He had searched the titles for that, and knew that Jeroboam, the second of that name, had been pleased with his work and had even put his name in the deeds as the consultant who had certified the religious correctness of this extension of Israel.

For Dove had been educated at Gath Hepher as a man of law.

A raindrop, from nowhere, plopped on the back of his hand.

In the school he had mastered the scrolls, but his heart was with the study of birds and plants. He had drawn greenshanks, buntings, and stonechats in the margins of his texts, the moabite sparrow, smew, stint, flycatcher, snipe, grebe, godwit, wheatear, moor hen, goldeneye.

He felt that he saw the Everlasting better in His creation than in the scrolls of the law. Angels had come down from the stars to men and women of old, and the Everlasting had dealt with Moses and Abraham face to face, a fire in a bush, a voice in the wind. But Dove preferred to know the Everlasting in the garden, the meadow, the terebinth grove.

The fair wind that had taken them from Joppa was beginning to blow hot, as from an oven, and then chill, as through a door opened in springtime. Sultry, then fresh. Fresh, sultry.

But the week before, of an evening, when he was admiring gourds in his garden, he had felt a voice at his ear. His astonishment was as great as his fear. There was no mistaking the voice. It was that of the Everlasting.

A merchant pointed out to another, and to Dove, a glow on the tip of the mast.

That fitful misty light was like the voice in the garden.

— O do not doubt but do believe!

— Lord I am not worthy.

— Thy name is the carrier dove.

The archaic Hebrew of the Everlasting with its purring gutterals and shimmering sibilants dropped word by word into his heart.

The wind fell calm, sails hung slack, the sea went flat.

— Go to Nineveh in Assyria, it said. Go to Nineveh in Assyria and take the people from their superstitions. Tell them that I am. Tell them fate is a lie. Tell them that I am that I am. Tell them that their images of monsters and wandering stars are but a pitiful and childish understanding of being.

It was in the cool after sunset, shadows filling the garden, doves cooing in the terebinths. He was admiring the small white gourds straked with bitter green, the longnecked gourds the color of sand, the martin's nest gourds. Cucumbers, gherkins, pumpkins.

It was old Liveforever, no doubt about it. *Jonah go to Nineveh in Assyria.*

He had done well to flee.

The sea began to heave in low greasy swells.

What had he to do with the dovecotes and bee gums of Assyria? The lions and hyenas of Assyria? They had Ishtar there, the abomination of the bed. Calculators of starlight, pounders of unlawful herbs, delineators of impossible creatures, bulls with wings, demons with claws.

The Everlasting is a spirit, source of our being, who guides the feet of the ant and the tooth of the fox, but man was left free to find for himself the hand of his maker. The swelling pumpkin sits while the vine on which it fattens creeps and multiplies its leaves. So the heart fills with knowledge as the body moves through the world, learning from kind and mean alike.

If the Everlasting made us free, why does he treat us like slaves?

There was a devil dance of lightning where a black wall of cloud sank down to the darkening sea.

— A squall, the captain said.

It hit so hard and so suddenly that the ship moved backwards. The sail tore loose and boomed above them. The sailors, each shouting to his god, began throwing bolts of merchandise into the sea. Some man, one said, with whom Baal is angry, is aboard this luckless ship. Another cried that someone who had done an unclean thing in the eyes of Thoth was with them. Who? The passenger Dove was asleep in a trance, some work of magic upon him.

The captain shook him until his head rolled on his shoulders.

— Is it you? he bellowed.

— He is the one! they all agreed.

— Is it you? the captain cried over and over.

— It is I, said Dove. I am a Jew. I am gripped by a great fear of my god, whose name is Everlasting, creator of the seas and the dry land.

— What can we do, a merchant asked, to keep your guilt from drowning us all?

And he said unto them:

— Take me up, and cast me into the sea. So shall the sea be calm unto you: for I know that for my sake this great tempest is upon you.

Nevertheless the men rowed hard to bring the ship to land, but they could not. For the sea worked against them. Wherefore they cried unto their gods, saying, Let us not perish because of this man, O Lord! Why should the innocent die in the loss of a sinner?

Then they hoisted Dove, three men carrying him, and threw him over the side.

Now the Everlasting had sent a great fish to swallow Dove, whose body was inside the fish for three days, but his face looked from the fish's mouth, and he held onto its back teeth. The fish leapt from wave to wave, and Dove breathed when the fish breathed, and held his breath when it swam under water.

I am, said Dove in his anguish, banished from the eyes of the Everlasting. I am dead, and yet alive. I exist, but the Everlasting is not with me.

I know what it is to exist and yet not be. I know how the roots of mountains and the bottom of the sea exist without knowing. I see that by putting myself and my comfort before the word of the Everlasting, I have abandoned mercy. I have made myself a stranger to kindness, and live in darkness, away from the light. My debt is enormous, but were I allowed to pay it, my thanksgiving would be endless, and I would pay beyond measure, again and again, without thought for anything else. For there is no life except that the Everlasting gives it.

And the Everlasting spoke a word to the fish, and it coughed Dove out upon the beach, where he danced with joy before he fell on his knees and prayed for hours and hours.

And a voice said again, *Jonah go to Nineveh that great city and preach as I told thee before to go and preach that I am and that I am that I am.*

Nineveh as all know is so wide a city that it takes three days to walk from the front gate to the back gate. When Dove was a day's walk into the city, confused by its booths and markets and temples that stank, he stood on a corner, in the dust, and shouted as loud as he could:

— Yet forty days, and Nineveh shall be overthrown!

People gathered about, and listened. They believed all he said, and repented, and wore sackcloth, and put ashes on their heads, from the king to the lowest beggar. The king sent an order throughout the city that the very oxen, asses, and sheep were to be dressed in sackcloth, and heaped with ashes, for the sake of repentance. Every word that Dove said, the king repeated as a royal decree. Every hand must stay itself in its violence, every heart must empty itself of lust. All the people of Assyria turned to the Everlasting, throwing their idols beyond the wall. Even then, the king was not certain that the Everlasting was not still angry unto death with him and his people.

But the Everlasting himself came as a voice to the king and said that he was pleased with him and his people, and would not afflict them with pestilence and earthquake after the forty days.

But Dove was filled with chagrin and outrage. He asked the Everlasting if he were sent as a prophet to destroy this wicked city, only to have his words cast back in his teeth, and his prophecy a mockery?

— Is it good to be angry? the Everlasting asked.

So Dove left the city, and pitched his tent outside the walls, for he believed in his heart that the Everlasting would strike the people with plague and a storm, and he wanted to see it, but not too close. He was happy when a gourd, his favorite of creation, grew before his eyes beside his tent. It grew faster than any plant outside Eden, by sinuous thrusts, putting out leaves like geese stretching their wings. In a matter of an hour the vine had made a green shade for Dove, and he sat in its cool with the sense that the Everlasting loved him, and had accepted his sorrowful repentance. Surely, on the morrow, Nineveh would perish, and Dove would be a prophet of great stature.

The morning came. Dove woke, and saw straightaway that his gourd vine was wilting. The cool wind of the morning turned hot. The vine drooped and died, its leaves turning brown before his eyes. Nineveh stood in all its splendor, going about its business as on any other day. Then Dove knew that the Everlasting was angry with him, and would do him a mischief again, and that Nineveh would not care one way or the other. I have, Dove cried, disobeyed the Everlasting and come within the width of a hair of death. And I have obeyed the Everlasting and come to humiliation. There is neither justice nor truth in the world, or in heaven.

As he sat in the broiling sun, he heard a voice in his ear.

— Is it good to be angry because the gourd withered away when you thought it was a sign of your triumph over Nineveh?

— It is good, said Dove in his anger. Would that I were dead.

— It is pity you feel for the gourd, the Everlasting said, because you loved it, and saw me in it. But there is not in you anything that can make a gourd to grow, to flower, to be fat with fruit. Nineveh is my gourd. I made her, that beautiful city. It is rich in cows, sheep, and oxen. And one hundred and twenty thousand people live there who cannot tell their right hand from their left.

The Ringdove Sign

• I

The Arctic Circle, Mariana said, and here's that light again. It's like nothing I've ever seen before. We're deep in conifers and aspen, and when their shadows begin to stretch out long, as now, all the hard accurateness of the light out here in the woods becomes this brilliant softness that lasts for hours, greens going blue, the sky violet, with neat lines of gold on the edges of things. Splendid is the word, Hugo said. And the midges dance out in hordes. Their jigs in spirals, their jigs in rounds. The gnats and leafhoppers here, Hugo said, are so many silly innocents compared to the ferocious samurai mosquitoes up north. On the Arctic Circle. You'd think the silence at the top of Sweden would be absolute. Not a bit of it. For one thing, the silence itself is an oppression, a density in the ear, so that the whine of mosquitoes and the hum of big black flies make a drone you wouldn't otherwise hear. We'd got to Boden by train, and marched out to the Circle in stages, great fun at that age. A devil, Mariana said. No I wasn't, I was sweet and shy. Ask Papa. We were joining a troop of Swedish Scouts, boys and girls together. A fine August day. For the North Pole. Which is considerably beyond, Smarty. On the Circle all the trees are dwarfs, as they grow so slow in that climate, getting root water only a few months of the year. Swamps of peat, fields of moss all warped and wavy. The evergreens are giving way to birches. When the Swedes saw our guidon down the path, the loneliest scraggiest worn path in the world, they turned out their brass band, and chose to greet us with *I Fratelli d'Italia*, Garibaldi's battle hymn, as handsome a piece as there is, always excepting *Wilhelm of Nassau*. I remember that the band all looked alike, peas in a pod, longish blond hair and cornflower-blue eyes, and almost uniform. The cornet was barefoot, and here and there one saw a shirttail out and an unbuttoned button, an unzipped fly, a haywire shoelace. But they played with spirit and dash, and to be met in that northern emptiness, that world of scrub and wild desolation, made us feel wonderful. We formed into a double file, and marched in to the music, left foot in time to the drum. Our scoutmaster, a freckly math teacher in steelrimmed specs and a race of coppery hair across his forehead, to be in style with his charges, saluted the Swedish master, or mistress, for she was a woman, and shook hands. The Swedes have the damnedest sense of humor. They told, over and over, with richer merriment every repeat, how the band got into its uniforms faster than it had ever before dressed, and how the trombone could not for the longest be found, and how they had a squabble as to whether they should play *King Kristian* or *Du Gamla, du Fria*, and compromised with Goffredo Mameli, as symbolic of idealism, youth, and liveliness. Mariana said, I've seen Franklin laugh at the bubbles in Perrier water.

• 2

When a mouse looks at the world, Einstein said, the world does not change. Yes it does, Niels Bohr replied. A little.

• LONG SHADOWS BEFORE THE FIRST STAR

The Summer Box, Papa calls it, Hugo said. I can remember talk as to whether it's a cabin or a hut. We came here for a month at least every summer, Papa and Mama (you would have liked her, and she would have liked you) and I, and on the odd weekend, when I could bring along a friend. The inconvenience of it is its charm for Papa, having to survive on what you bring. He divides people into those who like coming here and those who don't. Put me in the first lot, Mariana said. And Franklin and Pascal when they get here, day after tomorrow, isn't it? If they get on the right train, if they get on the right bus, if Pascal's folks delivered him at Papa's. Those two, Mariana said.

• BLUE RIVER WITH WILLOWS

My buddy Asgar and I were certain our scoutmaster was largely unacquainted with the female of the species other than his mother and aunts. He'd certainly never before seen a woman scoutmaster, especially one who laughed at the bubbles in Perrier water. It took a while to sort out the sex of the Swedish Scouts. They were all dressed exactly alike, had the same length of hair, and names weren't all that much help. A girl I thought for sure was a boy turned out not to be. We were supposed to communicate in Esperanto. We fell back on English. We pitched our tents in a line facing theirs and went off to a blue river lined by willows. There's no underbrush up there, no ferns like here, or berry bushes. Only moss, rock, stunted grass. The Swedish mistress said we must undress quickly and get into the water, or the mosquitoes would quite literally eat us alive. Was she ever right.

• TRACTATUS I.21

Any one fact can be the case, or not the case, and everything else remains the same.

• AUGUST

Hayfoot strawfoot, Hugo said, crunching larch cones, Pascal copying Franklin, off the forest trail to our campsite on the river. That's lovely, Mariana said, Pascal copying Franklin. I wouldn't have guessed that anybody would copy Franklin in anything. It's Franklin who's the champion copycat. After you appropriated me, which has, willy-nilly, involved appropriating Franklin too, he has taken you as the authority for all of life's surfaces and corners. He brushes his teeth, bathes, combs his hair. And now here's a well-off tyke at Grundtvig who seems to be the apple of his housemaster's eye and who talks like a book and as you've told me has the highest IQ in the school looking up to Franklin. Oh it's more than lovely, Hugo said. It began, you know, with that fight when Franklin took Pascal's side, wholly inexplicably, and then Holger asked me if I would take Pascal on an outing, to give him some sense of the practical and some measure of self-confidence. So when we had our tent pitched, the flaps reefed, and ringed rocks and set up a spit, we were in thick summer pastoral peace: frogs talking to each other across the river, a raven cawing, dragonflies glinting green. Pascal was whistling Mozart as we made camp, and so was Franklin, a musical ear I hadn't suspected. So the copycatting goes both ways. We'd crossed paths earlier on in the afternoon with some *Wandervögel* from Stuttgart, rather raunchily ahead of the times. One of them, sienna brown and as towheaded as an English sheepdog, eyes china blue, was wearing jeans shorts that would have fitted Franklin better, and their zipper was on the fritz so that the pod of his briefs, rusty yellow, stuck out through his fly. His girl, freckled pink and gold her whole face over, seemed to be wearing his shirt and nothing else. There were two boys in scarcely anything except packs and red caps who were holding hands. Another girl was sweetly barebreasted. They hailed us jovially. Pascal had questions, to which Franklin made up answers of an outrageous sort.

• 7

Tuesday, Mariana said, and whistled two long notes. I suppose the angels recorded it, they'd have to, blushing. If we came out here to love each other into fits and for you to pull together your crazy thesis, I hope the crazy thesis gets pulled together as well as the loving each other into fits. The angels won't blush, Hugo said. They probably wrote it out as music, or in annotations of which we know nothing. Or maybe as bald facts. Only hours after making love deep into a summer night, Hugo woke Mariana with his finger, causing her to talk salaciously in her sleep. Birdsong. A skimpy breakfast, after making love, scarcely interrupting renewed affections. Made love all morning. Lunch forgotten. Made love all afternoon. A walk in the meadow, naked as Adam and Eve.

• 8

Well, Pascal said once we were all shipshape with site and tent, as a matter of fact I call Housemaster Sigurjonsson Holger when we're by ourselves, never any other time. Hugo, Franklin said, is always Hugo. So, hr. Tvemunding, Pascal said, I'll call you Hugo. Very spadger, his ribs, with something baby bird in the shoulders, something goblinish about the back of the head. There was a tadpole flexibility before this gawkiness. A sturdy symmetry to follow. From Maillol to Soutine to Kisling. Franklin's a stage ahead with his prat pout and flat tummy, foxy eyes with the contour of an almond. Maillol, Hugo answered Mariana's question. Chloe. You are my goat, Mariana said.

• HYACINTHUS INDICUS MINOR

The root of this Iacinth is knobbed, like the root of arum or wakerobin, from whence spring many leaves, lying upon the ground and compassing one another at the bottom, being long and narrow and hollow-guttered at the end, which is small and pointed, no less woolly or full of threads than Hyacinthus Indicus Major. From the middle of these leaves the stalk rises long and slender, three or four foot long, so that without it be propped up, it will bend down and lie upon the ground.

• 10

Their two voices, Pascal's burgher correctness and school slang, Franklin's proletarian grittiness and complex grammar, began to swap locutions and tones. I adjudicated. I'll bet you did, Mariana said. Franklin said that I talk all sorts of ways, and that Pascal should hear me talking with my father, whom Franklin identified as a pastor and his personal friend. And that he should hear me talking with you. To barf, he added, immediately bragging about my teaching you English. I'm much more interested, Mariana said, in the Swedish Scouts at the North Pole, as I have a feeling that there was mousing from tent to tent in the night. There was no night, Hugo said. The sun stays up all day, sinking to the horizon and rising up again. The mosquitoes had attacked in rolling singing hungry swarms despite our nimble scramble into the blue river with willows, and we all smelled of witch hazel and iodine. Of course we had to sing folk songs around the campfire, eating ashy sausages. So, Mariana said, you began a life of tents and campfires. Did I? Hugo asked. Does that mean something? Deep in a forest makes for good talk and good fellowship. Objecting I wasn't, Mariana said.

• SILVER DRAGONFLIES

Holger says, Pascal said, we're all defeated by the inert violence of custom. This with a siffling sigh while Franklin was shedding every stitch. Shirt off, thrown down. A stare from me, a *sorry* from Franklin, and the shirt got hitched by its collar on the ridge pole. Pascal, imitating Franklin jot and tittle, doffed his togs. Blue Cub Scout short pants, identical as to red Swiss Army pocket knives pendant from belt loops, sheathed camping knives on left hip, canteen right hip, scut packs with nylon impermeables, compasses. Holger had seen to it that Pascal was to have precisely what Franklin was to wear right down to underpants (blushing), off, folded on mesial axis, and stashed in tent corner. It pleased Franklin to stomp around in shoes and socks only. This was when Pascal quoted Sigurjonsson quoting Sartre.

• 12

Perhaps what cannot be said is the ground on which what can be said comes by its meaning.

• BOEHME THE COBBLER

In some sense, love is greater than God.

• 14

Me, I'm simply lucky, Franklin said. Pascal munching a cinnamon bun at breakfast, up to his neck in my nylon parka, Franklin similarly engulfed in my khaki shirt but with his dinky maleness honestly bare, had said how keen it was to sleep in a tent and run naked and eat on a riverbank. Their wearing my parka and shirt referred to Franklin's saying that when he stayed over-night with us at NFS Grundtvig he wore my undershirt for a gown. Though it is always more probable that the reporter of a miracle has been deceived than that the miracle occurred, this does not obviate the miraculous, and there remains the space where the misunderstood has the force of miracle. There you go, Pascal said, using that word. What's wrong with it? Franklin asked. It's vulgar, is what, isn't it, hr. Tvemunding? Hugo, I mean. It's vulgar all right, I said, but it's Franklin's word. We are our words. We can, however, make the words we use, like poets and philosophers, and people who want to be understood. Most people are parrots, hoping to please by imitation. Squawk! said Franklin, and fell over backwards laughing at his own wit. Pascal waited two seconds before joining the laugh. Language, I persisted, always the explainer, is mostly a matter between friends, and friends can use words they wouldn't before some people, like parents and in public, on a bus, say. My language in class is impeccable, but gets saltier in the gym, looser at home. Holger, Pascal said, always talks the same. We're friends. Franklin gave one of his looks. Satiric doubt.

• THE MORE ANGELS, THE MORE ROOM

The second afternoon of an outing is when the roundness of it asserts itself. No need to tell me, Mariana said, shuffling into a dance and snapping her fingers. There's community, rhythm. The outside world has receded out of sight. Out of mind, Mariana said. There are no Kindergartens, no crayons stuck up noses, no peed knickers, no flash cards with Mina Jenssen croodling *dog* when I show the porcupine and *hat* for the letter A. The outside world has been replaced by an alternate one of exploring, swimming, botanizing, telling jokes, remembering analogues of each other's tales. I didn't think I'd like you at first, Franklin said to Pascal, but now I like you. Pascal thought of no reply, poor fellow. Well, Mariana said, a declaration of love from Franklin is not to be taken lightly. He didn't like you at first, was jealous, resentful. When the angels were manufacturing Franklin they broke off big blue pieces of heaven and worked them into his soul. Pascal too, Hugo said, but I don't think heaven has a great interest in mind, which is what the angelic craftsmen paid much attention to in Pascal. I asked myself what cautionary advice he'd had from Holger, who couldn't very well disapprove of Franklin. Probably some comprehensive warning against nastiness, certainly supererogatory in a school like NFS Grundtvig, but then Holger would have only a vague idea of townsfolk like you and Franklin. Who pinned Pascal's arms from behind and nuzzled his nape. Pascal froze, wriggled loose, and regarded Franklin with a look that slid to the tail of his eye. Whereupon Franklin, determined to hug somebody, came and hugged me. I was sitting, writing. I hugged back, and got to my knees and rolled him squealing over my head, and grappled him into a rolling hug that toppled us, and we fell knotted together arms and legs, hooting. Pascal, miserable, contracted his shoulders, one foot on top of the other. I swung Franklin loose, carried him by the armpits and stood him nose to nose in front of Pascal. You two, I said, work on your friendship. I've got notes to make, water to fetch, wood to gather, thoughts to think.

• SWEET YELLOW MOTH MULLEIN

The yellow moth mullein whose flower is sweet has many hard grayish green leaves lying on the ground, somewhat long and broad and pointed at the end: the stalks are two or three foot high, with some leaves on them, and branching out from the middle upwards into many long branches, stored with many small pale yellow flowers of a pretty, sweet scent, stronger than in other sorts, which seldom give seed but abide in the root, living many years.

• 17

Sunlight, once, on their tousled heads beyond the rocks downriver, their voices from the larchwood. Franklin kneedeep in sedge and wild carrot by a granite rockface spritted with mica and dappled with lichen was inviting Pascal to test the rigidity of his penis. O boy, Mariana said, trust my Franklin. I whistled my arrival. Franklin said brightly that they'd seen a badger trot and a grebe. Saw a water rat! Pascal said. The grebe had a golden craw with silver dots. Franklin was full of himself, talking big. I mussed both their heads, remarked that they were in the Serengeti of the saw-toothed chigger, and wanted both of them to soap up at the river, giving particular effort to their legs, and to smear themselves with insect repellent afterwards. Franklin boasted of an infestation of chiggers the summer before. This, he said, is my whatevereth camping trip. He'd been with me and you, and with the Cubs, and once with my troop. I'm the mascot. Sleep in Hugo's tent, march with him at the head of the column. But I like this better, friends only. Hugo studies God, and is the Greek, Latin, and gym teacher. Thanks, said Pascal, I only go to NFS Grundtvig. I forgot, Franklin said. Holger teaches biology and geography. He's been to Sicily and Iceland. Frogs and maps, Franklin said. Mitochondria and tectonic plates, said Pascal. Hugo's twice as old as me plus a year, Franklin said, and has been fucking since fifteen. His dick's 23 cm. He and my sister Mariana do it every day, because they love each other. Hugo's papa, he's a pastor in the Protestant cult, says it's kin to loving God, who wants us all to love each other. And then Franklin gave Papa a grand rating as a very bright old gentleman, pink and scrubbed, nattily dressed, who lives in a big old house with a flower garden all around it, and hundreds and hundreds of books inside, all of which he has read. Wise, generous, and liberal, especially in the matter of boys' monkeying with their peters, which is nature, and nature has God for its designer. Franklin omitted the detail of our visit when Franklin came down to breakfast britchesless and upstanding, and got a kind lecture on the way back upstairs, led by the hand, on conventions, decency, and several other matters. Ah yes, Mariana said, and that's when we heard the little twerp saying that you go around your apartment in nothing but an undershirt and me in nothing at all. I loved your father saying, yes but you'll notice they don't do that here, and they do it because they're very much in love with each other. Mercifully we didn't overhear the rest of the discussion.

• CLOVER. BUTTERFLIES

Not so silly fast, one heard Franklin from the far side of the tent. Like this, if you want it to feel good. At supper they sat shoulder to shoulder, shoving from time to time, with silly smirks. Holger, Pascal said, is shy. He starts to say things, and stops, changing the subject. The water rat was just along the river, where he has a trot like the badger's. Did you know that spiders rebuild their web every day? They eat it at night. Crazy, Franklin said. I hope we hear the owl again. Over the frogs. Don't they ever sleep? When Mariana and me are spending the night, Franklin said to me, can Pascal come over? We could make a pallet on the floor. Thing is, he said to Pascal, is not to be in the way, to move with, like a dog, and not against. Then we won't be underfoot. In wintertime we eat around the fire, like we're doing now. Fried bananas with brown sugar Mariana makes sometimes for a snack at bedtime. With milk. Did, I asked, Pascal like the idea? If so, I could square it with Holger. Pascal, shy, said nothing. What if Holger says I can't? he eventually said. But, I said, it was Holger who thought up this outing, after this rascal Franklin batted his eyes at him one day and said God knows what. Did I? Franklin said. Casually, calmly. The kid is on his way to being one of the world's great actors. O yes, that. I'll come, Pascal said, looking up brightly.

• 19

But why didn't you tell me, Mariana asked, about this light? And the moths and butterflies and the meadow over the hill? Privacy to love ourselves into fits, yes, and roughing it on the provisions we bring in, and water from a spring, and a cryptogonadal eleven-year-old with an IQ bigger than yours, and my idiot little brother, when they find us, and your father, in time, but not the magic soft long goldeny light. Which, Hugo said, will eventually last all night. That is, it will be the night. I'm not leaving it, Mariana said. I want to live with it, on it, in it, the rest of my life. I must, Hugo said, take you to the Arctic Circle, and maybe this time I won't be bitten by mosquitoes all over my virile member. Asgar, too. Which we made worse by whacking off as usual before falling asleep. Though it would have swollen up and turned purple all the same, I suppose. It was brave Asgar who boldly pulled his pants down for the Swedish scoutmistress next morning when she was daubing mosquito bites. Oh dear, she said, oh dear, what a frightfully awkward place to be bitten so cruelly. But she daubed away, with several other wounded, girls too, looking on with curiosity having overcome every scruple.

• THE BALLOON

It was over the meadow beyond the birchwood, descending, its gaudy colors, like those of a circus wagon, splendidly strange against the blue haze of the sky and the soft greens stitched with purple and yellow runnels of wildflowers in the meadow. The wooden paddles of the propeller were idling over. The telescope in its sweep flashed a white disc of glare. The *Jules Verne* was back, here.

• CLEMENT TO THEODORE

Add to the evangelium of Marcus: They arrived in Bethany where there was a woman whose younger brother had died. She found Yeshua and lying face down before him said *Son of Dawidh take mercy on me.* Those who were with Yeshua, his followers, spoke harshly to her, which angered Yeshua, who went with her to her brother's tomb in her garden. There they heard a loud voice from within the tomb, and Yeshua lifted aside the stone door, and went in, and took the young man in his arms. He sat him on the coffin's edge and took both his hands in his, and the young man looked at Yeshua and loved him, and begged that he might be with him always. They left the tomb and went into the house of the young man, who was rich. Now six days later Yeshua asked the young man to come to him at night, naked except for a linen cloth. And throughout the night Yeshua explained to him how the world had God for its king, and at morning Yeshua left Bethany and walked to the other side of the Jordan.

• MARCUS XIV: 51

Adulescens autem quidam sequebatur eum amictus sindone super nudo: et tenuerunt eum: at ille reiecta sindone, nudus profugit ab eis.

• SANKT HIERONYMUS WITH OPOSSUM

A sequence of twelve photographs by Muybridge: a dappled horse named Smith with rider, nude. A lithograph of 1887, the flat carbon of its blacks and silvery graphite of its half tones having the authority of both science and art. Smith's tail has dashed into an upward spray by the sixth photograph. The sequence records a single four-legged step, or, in horseman's language, stride. Time lapse between exposures: .051 seconds.

• 24

There was a dialogue conducted by the furniture, as in a De Chirico, where *Stimmung*, or time with the feeling of music, involves one thing with another, Mariana's flowery scarf, its Indian pinks, mustard browns, and Proustian lilacs, with the feral cunning of the large photograph framed in thin aluminum on the wall of Bourdelle's *Herakles Drawing His Bow*, Hugo's running shoes, their incisive blue stripes slanted like the insignia of a rank coparcenary with the god Hermes, coffee mugs in an event with light, a map of the Faeroes on the wall opposite the *Herakles*, a blue javelin standing in the northwest corner, a Cub Scout neckerchief, yellow and black, Franklin the Electrical Beavertooth Rabbit's, a vase of zinnias, a trapezoidal shaft of soft late afternoon from the skylight to the blue rug, the bed made as neatly as one in a barracks.

• MARCUS X:46

[They came to Jericho and the sister of the young man whom Yeshua loved and his mother and Salome were there, but Yeshua would not see them.]

• 26

Linen is the clue, Hugo said. Johannes the Dipper wears animal skins: that seems to be very important, and when Yeshua is mocked and tortured he is made to wear a purple emperor's robe, to satirize what they think are his pretensions to being a ruler. But otherwise he wears linen. *Byssos*, the garb of Pythagoreans and the Essenes. Angels wear white linen: that's standard. A pure garment: animals have not been slaughtered to make it. And as the tomb on Easter morning, linen linen linen, flashing white, pure. A daimon would wear linen when he is apparent to the eyes of the vulgar in this world, though the structural detail is for the daimon to be naked, like the infant Yeshua, signifying sinlessness. And, Mariana said, her chin on her knees, looking out into the beautiful northern twilight, you think that the gospel writers could not wholly detach themselves from the ancient and pervasive Mediterranean belief in daimons as angelic messengers from heaven to an inspired person, a philosopher or a teacher like Yeshua, and gave him one: he's the adolescent naked except for a piece of linen in the scene of the arrest, and he's the younger brother Yeshua revives and talks to all of a night, and he's the angel at the tomb on Easter. He's all over the place, Hugo said. The revival in the garden has come down to us folklorishly askew. The chap's name was El'azar, or Eleazar, on in Latin Lazarus. Check out daimons with names, like angels. The night's conversation ought to be messages from on high for Yeshua, not Yeshua instructing a rich young man whom he has brought back from the dead. He's also probably the same as the rich young man Yeshua said should give all he had to the poor. And, Mariana said, these things got scrambled around in the writing. First in the telling, Hugo said. Each early community would have had its own history, and over a hundred years details transmute. I tell you an interesting story, but you don't quite get the drift of all of it. You then repeat the story, and account for certain details in your own way, or the way you understood them. A hundred years pass. Versions get written down, some of them in languages not one's native tongue. You see? And the daimon had, in one of the longest traditions we can trace in the Mediterranean, a bird form. A dove. More than any other folktale, Yeshua mentions the sign of Jonas. That is, the sign of the dove. Jonas means dove, Mariana said. I do listen. You're better at this than I am, Hugo said.

• THE BOW OF HERAKLES

Up these outside steps, Franklin said. Hugo lives here. It was the top floor of the stables, way back, now a garage and place where the grounds people keep their things. Somebody, a teacher here, who left, he taught drawing and building houses and things, made the upstairs one big room, but with a bathroom and kitchen and a skylight. When Hugo came here, all he needed was a bed and a chair and a table to make himself a place to live. Pots and pans and things. Hugo says that what you own should be a pair of jeans, shoes, socks, and shirt. One sweater. But he only talks that way. He has lots of things. This, around my neck on this shoelace, is the key. Mariana has one, too. You first. That big picture, it's a photograph of a statue in Paris Frankrig, where Hugo bought it. He's been all sorts of places. Greek, Pascal said, a hero from the myths. Yes, said Franklin, you see he was good and strong and he shot bad things with his bow, things that hurt people. He's naked because the *Grækere* didn't wear any clothes most of the time, big balls like Hugo's, but this picture here, which Hugo painted, of my sister Mariana, is naked because girls are pretty with no clothes on. Hugo can paint real good. He has drawn me all sorts of ways, with color pencils, my pecker on view, chinning a limb down by the river, asleep in that chair. A Muybridge, Pascal said, looking at the photograph in twelve frames of the horse Smith. Brancusi's *Torso d'un jeune homme*. Hugo says that has purity, whatever the fuck he means by that. Pascal winced. Now I've said something wrong, Franklin said. Let's have a glass of milk. The *Torso* is beautiful, Pascal said. It has elemental simplicity. In the archaic Mediterranean period the body was shaped that way in Cycladic and Maltese sculpture. Cycladic, Franklin said, Cycladic. Here, Pascal said, taking down a book and flipping through the pages. There, he said, that's Cycladic. You knew it was in that book? Franklin asked. No, but by the title there was a good chance. You could have said you knew it was in the book and fooled me. I don't want to fool you, Pascal said. Good milk. Franklin drank his at a go, and licked the inside of the glass held upside down. As he licked, he squeezed the crotch of his short white pants. Pascal sat in Hugo's reading chair, feet and all, ankles crossed, and sipped his milk. What I think, Franklin said, unzipping, is that you're not balls up inside anymore. It didn't look like it when we were camping with Hugo. You get stiff good. And you say it feels neat to play with it. If it feels half as good as mine, you're getting there. Why would your housemaster friend Holger say you can whack off in moderation if he doesn't want you to do it at all, you know? See, one pull back and one pull up, and I'm bone-hard and tingling. Pascal spilt a fat dollop of milk on his shirt and pants. Fuck, Franklin said. Don't get it on the rug. Here, over to the sink. Shirt, britches: rinch 'em in cold water, is what Mariana would do. They'll be dry again in no time. Underpants, too. Your dick's half stiff, you know. What, Pascal said, if hr. Tvemunding comes in, or your sister? What nothing, Franklin said. You don't know those two. They don't think about anything else. And they don't snitch. See, pull back, slide up. Everybody at Grundtvig whacks off two or three times a day. I know that, Pascal said. In the showers, in bed, up over the boathouse. Yours has a more mushroomy head than mine. See, I'm getting hair. Hugo's has big veins all over it, and bumpy ridges. Long as my forearm, and the head's as big as my fist. See, he said he got it that big by whacking off when he was a boy.

• 28

Do you, Pascal said, know about the nest of crystals in a salmon's brain by which it steers in a magnetic field? Like a radio, said Franklin.

• 29

The peaches, Mariana said, have been in the spring, in their tin, and so's the condensed milk, which is why they are so delicious and Hugo is smiling at me with designs in his eyes. One design. All the writing's to be done by the time Papa gets here, so that he can read it through. He's going to like the hobbyhorse. And the structuralist analysis of clothes. Wheat and figs will be nothing new to him, or Gnostic static.

• THE GREAT APPLE ROSE

The stock is large, covered with a dark grayish bark except for the younger branches, which are reddish, armed here and there with great and sharp thorns, but nothing so great or plentiful as in the Eglantine, although it be a wild kind: the leaves are whitish green, almost like the first White Rose, and five always together, seldom seven: the flowers are small and single, consisting of five leaves, without any scent, or very little, and a little bigger than those of the Eglantine bush, and of the same deep blush color, every one standing upon a prickly button, bearded in the manner of other roses, which, when the flowers have fallen, grow great, long and round, pear-fashion, bearing beards on their tops and are very red when full ripe.

• ACORNS

Earliest dawn, mist, the shine of dew, a single star still in the sky. Hugo could make out the basket of the *Jules Verne* in an open place in the pines, its rope ladder down. Quark, he called softly. Quark, again. He heard a voice speaking God knew what language: it was more animal than human, full of chirps and ratchety gutturals. He called again. Ferns parting before him, a boy naked as a newt, wet to the hips, strode out with wide rolling steps, waving his arms in greeting. It's you, he said. Can we talk? Hugo said. Talk? Quark said. You *are* Quark? Hugo asked. There were the three of them, ten or eleven in age, Quark, Buckeye, and Tumble, voyagers in a balloon of the last century. We are washing in the dew, Quark said, and drying in the air. It's wonderfully *so me tumenge 'kana rospxenava ada zhivd'ape varikicy romenge*, Buckeye! you worthless goosebrained chickenhumper, put me back onto Danish. He fiddles with the adaptors on the thread out of absolute gormless idleness. *El ruaus della dumengia damaun fa*, stop it! Buckeye's radiantly grinning handsome face rose over the wicker taffrail of the basket. I was getting us all into *lingua loci*, Crosspatch, while heating the griddle for pancakes, and reading the newspaper we bought in the village. Hi, Hugo, what brings you out to the ship so early of a morning? Tumble is out milking cows. A little from several: so it won't be missed. Pancakes, blackberries, and milk. Who are you? Hugo asked. Not to say, said Quark. What language is your name?

Quark looked blank, smiling. Buckeye! he called. Ask Hizqiyya Band yot asterisk scanner to give us a printout in Latin letters quote what language is your name close quote, with *your* referring to Zoon Hex Dyo Hen. Tapped in, Buckeye called down. Green through, red active, here it comes. Here it is. QUARK ULT QUERCUS LATIN OAK EVANGEL DODONA CROSSREF IRISH THEOLOGER JAMES JOYCE CRY OF GULL ARCHETYPE DOVE SIGNUM JONAS ALSO CROSSREF ELEM PARTICLE SYNERGIA MUNDI CROSSREF HARMONY BROTHER BUCKEYE MT OAK GENUS AESCHYLUS OR BUCKEYE TREE ALSO CROSSREF BROTHER TUMBLE FREQ GALLIC TOMBER ENGL TIMBER CROSSREF TREE SYMBOL CONNEC VAR MY-THOLOG DRYAS DAIMONES REQ ROUTES REMIND YOU RESTRICTED EXCEPT DESIGNATE POETS PS HIZQIYYAH TO PATROL WHO WANTS TO KNOW?

• BOULDERS SEAMED WITH GOLDEN SAMPHIRE

Looking out of the top of his eyes, whistling Mozart, Franklin unlatched the buckle of his Wolf Cub webbing belt, fingered the brass button from its eye, and slid his zipper down. Get chiggers on your behind and balls, Hugo said, if you're about to do what I think you're about to do. Which is what? Pascal asked. I can read Franklin's mind, Hugo said. Several meters back, on the flint path, the Electric Rabbit's paw was squeezing its crotch, and now its unwrinkled brain slips along an obvious and wholly natural line. That's not my mind you're reading, Franklin said. A joke, Pascal said. I'm learning.

• A GARDEN IN POMPEII

With a stone Hercules in it, Buckeye said. At one end, where the olive a hundred years old was. And at the other, with the seedlings in perforated jars, the bee balm, polpody fern, amaranth and bachelor buttons, was a stone Priapos. Rose, white violet, dogtooth, wallflower, Tumble said, bergamot, thyme, saffron crocus. The Perfumery of Herakles was the sign above the door, across from the shop whose sign was Cash Today Credit Tomorrow. For cool and colors and smell you would have to go to Kyoto or Izmir to find the like. The dog Ferox, remember him? They'd sawn an amphora in half, on the long axis, and one half was his bed, the other, on stacked bricks, his roof. There was another grand garden at the House of the Ship *Europa*. A stone Ceres. Demeter of the Campania. And up here, peppergrass, so sour and green.

• ANEMONE

Wheat figured in gold on the steel blade of his sword, in sudden windflowers that came with the rain, clad in white linen, Hyakinthos.

• BLUE-EYED SUSANS

To the reedy plangencies of a harmonium from Sheffield (John Robinson, Instruments, 1869) Buckeye sang *O lead me onward to the loneliest shade.* Sing through your nose, Quark said, with quavers and shakes. That's the way *they* do it. By gaslight in the Methodist Chapel. *The dearest place*, Buckeye obliged, *that quiet ever made.* Holy milk cow, Tumble called up from the meadow below. *Where kingcups grow most beauteous to behold, and shut up green and open into gold.*

• EPPING FOREST 1840

I found the poems in the fields and only wrote them down.

• 37

Pascal's folks, Pastor Tvemunding said, thought it would be best if I came with them, and here we are, ready for anything. Mariana, Hugo said, heard you first and is exchanging Eve's dress for modester raiment. Well, Pastor Tvemunding said, you were allowed to run naked here as a boy, even after you qualified for the *toga virilis*. There's not a soul in miles. How come, Franklin said, after being kissed on the top of the head, forehead, and chin by Hugo, Hugo can be naked and Mariana not? Answer that, Mariana said from somewhere in the cabin, and lots of other answers will follow. Papa Tvemunding, hi! Tailless rats, hi! You've all three turned up together, what fun. She's going to kiss you, Pascal, Franklin said. So kiss back.

• THE TWELVE DAYS

The *kallikantaroi*, daimons or perhaps centaurs (the Greeks still believe in them), were loose on middle earth, from underneath, for the twelve midwinter days, playing havoc. If they could be appeased and sent back to the underworld, the new year could begin. They were horses, or halfhorse halfhuman, ithyphallic, unprincipled and raw. The Greeks, even so far back in time, had the sense that life was wild impulse that needed taming, needed synchronicity, regularity, rhythm. Noise must become music, sexuality a longing of affinities, violence government, babble poetry, wild grass wheat, fear of the inexplicable religion, the puzzle of the world philosophy. But the romping centaurs have stayed on, in rituals all over Europe, and the dance of the hobbyhorse is their last vestige. At the beginning they are indistinguishable, let us surmise, with the idea of daimons in general: spirits who possess or guide or tempt. Tell you about the hobbyhorse? Well, it's man in a horse suit, many variants. He does a dance in which he gets sick and falls down. A lady horse comes and revives him with her attractions. Then something that was wrong has been set right again. Springtime can come. Crazy, said Franklin. Folklore, said Pascal. Neat, said Mariana. I think I see what you mean, said Pastor Tvemunding.

• 39

With a floppy and sidewise gait, goofy of eye and with idiot teeth, an agile cripple, sinking in his pace, the hobbyhorse falls down. Poor. Old. Tired. Horse. Doctors try pills and enemas. The old horse moans, the old horse groans, like to die. This is the one dramatic role rustics up and down the map get to play. They practiced their reins, their careers, their prankers, their ambles, their false trots, and Canterbury paces. They wore horse bells, plumes, and braveries, and bragged in the opening dance to tabors and fifes, bagpipes and clacker sticks, of having a mane new-shorn, and frizzled, and of having a randy wayward giddy leaning toward the tupping of a mare. And dances himself silly. He falls. The women show him eggs. But he is old, he is tired. Hope on High Bomby he is not, nor a coach horse of the Pope, who can mount thirty mares one after the other, whickering and neighing, with his black yard still hard as a hoe handle, his tail waggling, a fine roll to his handsome eye, and his ballocks throbbing with lewdness. Oh no, that's all past. He's a sick old horse fallen in the road. But then a young mare is brought for him to see. He looks, he neighs Whee Hee. The mare says Tee Hee.

• 40

The daimons, Papa Tvemunding said, were the agents of Fate. It is my understanding that Yeshua cancelled Fate.

• 41

Oh no! Franklin said. Not Sunday School out here! It's all a blur, Pascal said. Hugo said, Use your imagination. Olive groves. The olive leaf is dark green on top, light grayish green on its underside. So if there's a breeze, you see sudden, rolling, tossing changes of color. Like foam on breakers at the shore. I'm seeing it, Franklin said, closing his eyes. Me too, Pascal said. OK then, Hugo went on. Yeshua. Hair probably black, black and shiny with perfumed oil. Sidelocks in curls down by his ears. A hat? Yes, let's give him a big round straw hat, shallow-crowned, for walking in the broiling sun. A beard. Imagine him as a comely man, wonderfully attractive, big-nosed, very Mediterranean. Tall and sturdy: he was a carpenter. Though God knows, for all we're told, he could have been chubby and bald. Big floppy trousers, like a Turk, or modern Cretan. Sandals. And a kind of coat: a caftan, I suppose. He would have spoken Aramaic, and probably Greek. That was the common-market language of the Roman empire. He could read Hebrew, which no one any longer spoke: we see him doing it in the synagogue.

• A ROW OF ZINNIAS

Listen to the ringdove, Pastor Tvemunding said. It's the angle of light in its retina, Hugo said. They'd brought a table out on the meadow where it flows into the cabin's grounds. Wonderful that you brought tea, Mariana said. Hugo never thinks to. These intellectuals assume everybody likes coffee. What a glorious, sweet afternoon. I hear more than ringdoves, I hear unchanged voices over in the larchwood. Happy voices, Pastor Tvemunding said. Hugo, I've read far enough into your thesis to see that the faculty is going to adjust its glasses page after page, wondering if it's reading what it's reading. But I imagine they'll kick through with a degree. I like it. It stands to reason that something so universal in Mediterranean belief as daimons would get into the gospels, and be removed, except for the traces you indicate, by scribes who didn't understand what they were excising. There was the worship of angels at Kolossai. Your theology is going to be carped at. You require an organism for spirit, allowing for no occurrence of mind except in something, even if it be an organization of matter still unrecognized by science. And you allow for no knowledge of the future in the mind of God, as the future hasn't yet happened, and is not something of which there can be any knowledge. That's good logic, isn't it? Hugo asked. Yes, his father said. Sounds absolutely useless to me, Mariana said. Hugo, what are you looking at? The light, he said. He was looking at Quark in a French sailor's suit, standing behind his father. He gave Hugo a wink, which meant: Nobody but you can see me. He mouthed *light frequency*. He sniffed the teapot, and signalled for Tumble, whose slender honeybrown body was clad only in briefs which Hugo had last seen on Franklin. Buckeye was probably on the roof of the cabin: he dared not look. The whole crunch of theology, he said, is to what extent do people imagine that creatures of another realm, higher or lower, or invisibly within ours, interact with our lives?

• GUYOT, 1900

It is not enough to describe, without rising to the causes, or descending to the consequences. A complete account of vision would contain far more than a description of the sequence of chemical reactions that begins when a rhodopsin molecule absorbs a photon.

• SCALIGER ON ACTS XVII:18

Ethnici non credebant diabolum esse; Socratis daemonium vel deum vel genium esse credebant.

• 45

Steam seeping from the brass throttle, the red lantern glowing brighter as the dusk thickened to dark, the balloon eased to fifty meters above the larchwood, most of which was already in deep green night, with some clearings and tall trees still suffused with the last thin pink of sunset. Buckeye, pushing back his Norwegian forager's cap on his curls, tried another sip of coffee. *They* drink it, he said. It's a bean, Tumble explained, from a beautifully slender tree in the Indian Ocean islands. It came up here over long trade routes years and years ago. The bean's roasted and then ground, sometimes powdered. Hot water makes it into a tisane. Add granulated cane sugar, and it's a drink. Tastes more than a little of lion piss, wouldn't you say? Ah, but the bouquet, the aroma, Quark said, rolling himself into his blanket for the night. Hugo the theologer likes it, and his da. Mariana pretends to like it. Tumble pretends to like it. I *do* like it, Tumble protested. HQ, you know, isn't really interested in this bunch. A cute old man, his tall randy son who can't keep his generator in his pants, one sprightly girl and her little brother, and his friend. So Hugo is writing some gibberish, and teaches the old languages, which he mispronounces, and has a loving heart, what's the bother? Pass the molasses cookies. Maybe it's all for Pascal, Buckeye said. He's the deep one.

• A GARDEN IN POMPEII

Hello, Quark said. He was behind a beech, looking around. Hugo saw a portion of blue student cap, an eye, a quiff of hair. Where is the balloon? Hugo asked, and then in a temper, why do you bother with it? Asking questions won't do, Quark said, trying to be very serious. Be silent, be bold, be of great heart: that's the message. But the other morning, Hugo said, you talked to me about Pompeii, the old olive, the dog. You cannot imagine what curiosity you excite. We can't read minds, Quark said. We got an *admonitum* on the thread for talking too much, and for borrowing Franklin's underpants. From whom? Hugo asked. What's on the other end of the thread? The *Consiliarii*. Hugo looked more puzzled than ever. We have only heard their voices, Quark said. They give us messages to deliver, charges to look after, things like that. Where are you when you aren't here? Hi! said Tumble, looking around the other side of the beech. Where are we when we aren't here? I wonder if we know. It is left to us to rig out our expeditions. We got the balloon out of a book of pictures, and we get our clothes where we can, and our food, as when we're inside a system we have to live in its structure. Are you always ten-year-old boys? Oh no, Tumble said. We have been wolf puppies when a mother lost hers. Dolphins. Magi from Persia. Watch it, Quark said. We don't remember all of our assignments. And once they're done, it wasn't us, somehow, who did them, you know? Actually, Tumble said, they keep things from us, practically everything I sometimes think. Pompeii, Hugo said, to hold onto that, because you remember it. Do you know what happened to it? Happened to it? Quark asked. Our information, like yours, as best we can tell, is not magic, as your language has that word. Did something happen to Pompeii? Have you no way, Hugo asked, of finding out?

• 47

I agree with you, dear Mariana, Papa Tvemunding said, about the light up here. It finds something in our souls. As for Hugo's youthful adventures on the Arctic Circle, I imagine the version I got years ago, as it must seem to you, but only yesterday to me, Hugo has grown up so swiftly, is slightly different from the one you've heard. I'm fascinated by what you tell me about little Pascal. A kind of genius, is he? And for Franklin, my charming Franklin, to be bringing him out: that's a sweet wonder. I have had an entire troop of Scouts suddenly fill the house, when Hugo had the prescience to march them in. Once, even, when Margarita was alive. Tents in the garden, bedrolls on every floor.

• FICUS

All three kinds of fig trees are in leaves and growing one like another, save for their height, color, and sweetness of the fruit, having many arms or branches, hollow or pithy in the middle, bearing very large leaves divided sometimes into three but usually into five sections, of a dark green color on the upperside, whitish beneath, yielding a milky juice when it is broken, as the branches also or the figs when they are green: the fruit breaks out from the branches without any blossom, contrary to all other trees of our orchard, being round and long, shaped like a small pear, full of small white grains, of a very sweet taste when it is ripe, very mellow, and so soft that it cannot be carried far without bruising.

• 49

Come up! Buckeye called down to Hugo. You can see the nacelle, the engine. Hugo, naked as Tarzan, had come out early to walk around the woods, as he always did of a morning. The balloon was suddenly above him before he was aware that it was anywhere near. Up he climbed, feeling giddy as the rope ladder swung away, rung by rung, and began to sway wildly before he reached the taffrail. Tumble and Quark were still rolled up in a blanket, arms around each other. I'm on watch, Buckeye explained. Quark woke, grinned, disentangled himself from Tumble and the blanket, impulsively gave Hugo a kiss and hug, and went to the taffrail to pee over the side. Hugo took in the strangeness of the nacelle: the brass-and-walnut levers, the Edisonian phone and telegraph, the neat cabinets, steam gauges from the age of Isambard Kingdom Brunel, and none of this was out of style with the Danish togs draped over ropes, American jeans, French underpants, Finnish sweaters, an Italian coffeepot. Breakfast, Tumble said, his thick hair a wreck, eyes sleepy. Croissants, to be heated in the engine. Espresso. Fig jam, from the country store over the hill. Butter. The four of them sitting, knee against knee, filled the floor of the basket, with room for cups and saucers in the ring of their toes. I can't stay long, Hugo said. They're beginning to wonder about it all. Pompeii, Quark said. You asked. We asked. They have the records at HQ. They have everything at HQ, if you know who to ask. It's awful. There was a day, I forget the coordinates, when the sky was all white, which was dust and smoke, and then it was yellow, slowly turning black. This was the volcano Vesuvius, it had erupted. Ashes in the air, miles high, which sifted down for days on the garden on the Via Nuceria, so deep that it covered the great olive, and Ferox's doghouse, the flowers, the very roofs. A flower garden one day, an ash heap the next. Fig jam and butter, Tumble said, they tickle the back of the throat. But I knew that, Hugo said. Then, Buckeye said, why did you ask us to find out?

• A BLUE SUMMER SKY

Franklin! Mariana! Hr. Tvemunding! Hugo! Pascal said, running from the meadow. Up in the air! There's an absolutely scrumptious hot-air balloon over the larchwood. It's all decorated with signs of the zodiac, and circus colors, and fancy patterns. I waved, and whoever's in it waved back. They were hauling in an anchor, so they must have been tethered over there. Hurry, or you'll miss it.